Sleep Decades

Sleep Decades

stories

Israel A. Bonilla

Sleep Decades is a work of fiction.

©2024 Israel A. Bonilla

Quotations for review/scholarly purpose and falling within the guidelines of fair use are welcome.

ISBN: 979-8-9903240-1-5

Cover design by David Wojciechowski.

Published in the United States of America by Malarkey Books.

malarkeybooks.com

A grateful acknowledgment to the following magazines, which first published the specified pieces:

BULL: "Love—" and "Boca de Iguanas."
New World Writing: "Basement Blues."
En Bloc: "A Threefold Cord."
King Ludd's Rag: "Confessions of an American Marihuana User."
Damnation: "Roulette."
Tilted House Review: "As the Waters Fail from the Sea."
Berfrois: "Antisophers."
A Thin Slice of Anxiety: "Margins."
Exacting Clam: "Remnant."
Minor Literature[s]: "Bloom."

*And we feel, day and night,
The burden of ourselves—*

Matthew Arnold

A Biography in Ten Objects	11
Draft	23
Alive and Well	29
A Threefold Cord	43
As the Waters Fail from the Sea	51
Antisophers	55
All the Works That My Hands Had Wrought	71
Remnant	83
Roulette	91
Boca de Iguanas	95
Love—	101
Luna, Agueda, Lulú	107
Bloom	117
Loneliness by the Window	121
Confessions of an American Marihuana User	131
Basement Blues	147
Margins	151
Levity	157
τὸ ὄν	163

A Biography in Ten Objects

REPRESENTING a life involves many forms of treason. It is easy to latch onto things that prove our fine-spun theories. There is even a measure of gusto in declaring irrelevant what is taken for granted and revealing an unknown person: he was not, actually, a man of faith; she was not, to be true, an altruistic woman. We always believe to have some insight alien to the sitter, to have some degree of detachment. And there is a tendency, no doubt, to emphasize embarrassment, humiliation, irrationality, as if the moments of weakness were characteristic precisely owing to their dearth.

Representing the life of a relative would seem to avoid these pitfalls. Too much closeness befalls us. Yet the supply of intimate details nourishes our hubris. We declare the real possibility of detachment, for we know just the spots where we should adjust our brush-stroke. So let me, at the outset, break with tradition—I am anything but detached to Gregoria Bazán. I will offer a glimpse of what she means to me in the manner of Vermeer—by a painstaking attachment to the everyday bric-a-brac. Maybe only thus can one speak of faithfulness.

Glasses

She's lying on the scarlet couch. Most of her face is stiff. Her lips, the exception, move in staccato. Every three or four minutes she pushes upward with her left index finger a random part of the temples. It's hard to tell whether this is a matter of comfort or of habit. The book on her lap is called *This Too Shall Pass*. It elicits nothing other than complete seriousness. I stare with a mixture of wonder and second-hand embarrassment. Is this utter abandon a respite close to meditation or pure play-acting? Given the iron hand with which she governs the house, I'm inclined toward the latter. I try and try to understand, but I feel uncomfortable whenever she reaches for her case. Two hours of silence is the norm.

We leave the house with the scarlet couch, we leave the little apartment that has walls as thin as silk, we leave the country, and the metamorphosis takes place without pause. But on the bus I begin to get the hang of it.

"You'll get bored if you don't read. Look, I think you'll like this."

The Knight in the Rusty Armor. I expect adventures; instead, I find some kind of marital disagreement. Since I don't want to disappoint her, I plod on. An adventure does materialize, and I end up turning the pages with a bit more enthusiasm.

"So? Did you like it?"

"There's a lot of talk."

"Yes. It's there because it has a message."

"That the knight doesn't need the armor."

"It's more than an armor!"

She messes my hair. Nothing else is said about the book.

A Biography in Ten Objects

Angel Lamps

Olive, our neighbor, extolled its wonders. This time, though, she left her merchant outfit at the door and put on that of the aesthete.

"It's beautiful. Just look at it. And we haven't even turned it on. Look at that! Exquisite. The colors, the movement. If I could have five more in my living room, I would, but I just couldn't stop thinking about you. 'Gregoria would love it. She's not like other clients. Only the good stuff with her.' But seriously, it's divine. Your living room would light up. By the way, I do have another one waiting in case your daughters are interested. Like mother, like daughter."

Olive didn't have to do the whole pitch. Gregoria's eyes were transfixed as soon as the lamp's flakes turned red, yellow, and blue. She bought both lamps, but never really told anyone that one was for sale. Each November and December she turns them on at night.

"They're very pretty, aren't they?"

"They're lamps. And were kind of pricey."

"That's not important. They're nice. The living room looks great. They're a perfect match for it."

She's leaving for the summer to take care of Don Eustacio. Trust has never been high when it comes to turning over the household. With the lamps, however, the word is meaningless.

"Listen to me. If you break one of those lamps, let alone both, we're going to have a serious disagreement."

"They'll be fine. I won't be playing with them or anything."

"You know what I mean. Have your parties, get drunk, whatever. I want those lamps intact, okay?"

"Yeah, all right. Worst-case scenario I pay you."

"No! It's not about money. How would you even pay me? No. Hide them if you must. I want to come back and see them in their place. Like new. You know what . . ."

Before I try to reassure her, she lets go of her baggage and starts to disconnect the lamps.

"I'll do it for you. Forget they exist."

"Give me a break."

"I mean it."

I laugh, but she is unrelenting in her solemnity.

Cell Phone

She keeps it in a drawer. When she leaves the house, she may or may not carry it. If I had to guess, she's received ten calls in these four years, only two of which she's answered. The grandchildren have saved it from musty oblivion. Perhaps they've done more than that—the notification sound has been ringing for days. At last, she asks for help.

"I'm done with the noise. Please stop it."

"You'll keep running into this problem. You can't keep handing them the phone."

"It's my phone, not yours."

"It's an easy fix. They just downloaded a useless app. But it'll happen every time you give it to them. Kids aren't smart with phones."

"Bah! I've seen them. They're smarter than you and me. I didn't ask for advice."

"Okay, fine. Then at least pay attention so you can do it on your own next time."

"I'm too old for that."

"My aunt is a consummate user. It would come in handy, you know. Both of you love to sneak around on Facebook."

A Biography in Ten Objects

"I refuse to become an addict. Is it so hard for you to help? You don't want a tally, believe me."

"There you go."

She inspects the phone, as if there were a way to assess my job through sheer intuition. There is a trace of amusement on her face.

"How can you waste so much time on this? I've been looking at it for a minute and my eyes already hurt."

The screen suddenly locks. She conceals her surprise. I sense, however, the disappointment.

Pen

It always stands guard on the bedside table. Sometimes sticky notes are near, sometimes an old planner with a bright-rose cover. I once had the idea that the former were used for cooking recipes while the latter was reserved for books. But no. She really has no system other than her pragmatic whim.

The pack of sticky notes gathers many aphorisms of a religious tint. Here's a representative sample:

—Don't try to change others if you haven't changed yourself first.

—There is no use in dwelling on the past. It is gone and no longer in your control.

—Forgive! Forgive! Only in forgiveness can repose be found.

—Speak to your inner child. Embrace it and nurture it. Let go of any shame.

—He listens. Though you may not understand the answer for now, be sure he listens.

The old planner is a bit more kaleidoscopic:

—Add one tablespoon of honey to your lemonade to calm that acid reflux.

—Meditate 1 hour a day. Get at least 15 minutes of outdoor light.
—I fear I'll die without reading all those piles on my bookshelves.
—Your child has his own life: respect it. Yours can be reworked indefinitely.
—Vinegar and baking soda can clean almost any surface!

I suspect they're all quotations. I've seen her more than once copying the words with care. To no avail, of course. Her penmanship is as childish and rushed as mine.

Shopping Cart

Rust overspreads at the bottom. A squeal escapes from one of the right wheels whenever it moves. The plastic handle is half broken. All in all, its deliverance is belated. But she takes it out for a ride two times a week. And she loads it as if it were brand new. There's enough confidence to convince me that it's no longer a matter of expediency. As she pulls it through the step of the entrance, it rattles and seems close to collapsing.

"What's with not buying a new one, eh?"

"What? And be like my sisters, buying and discarding things every month? No, thank you."

"You're as extreme. Not being them is the reason?"

"A car could run over it and everything remain the same. When I bought it, people still made things that would last. It just isn't like that anymore. My sisters were an example of how it all works now. That's it."

"I agree, but one day you're gonna get hurt, you know."

"My miquita rarely replaced her kitchenware. She used to say that only years of cooking gave them your side. It's the same here. This armatoste has my side."

She's sweating. I help her with the bags. As I haul the last one out, I notice a laminated painting of the Child of Atocha at the bottom.

"No one's getting hurt. My little boy wouldn't allow it."

Molcajete and Tejolote

They were the staple of our kitchen back when we lived in the house with the scarlet couch. I'd stop playing around and go watch her mash habaneros, chiles de árbol, pepitas, peppers, onions, garlic, tomatoes. However suspicious the mess, my taste would be happily overwhelmed. This tradition suffered a blow when Olive showed her the Royal blender.

"Oh, Goyita, you and your old ways. You'll save hours of your life. I know the number these molcajetes can do to your hands. And let me be perfectly clear: you have the most beautiful hands."

"That's very kind, but I already have one."

"So out of date, Goyita, that you might as well have none. You can't match the Royal blender. Don't you have problems with the blades?"

"Yes, they can be a headache sometimes."

"There it is."

But it wasn't dealt a fatal blow. She's preparing cochinita pibil, and though at first she puts an habanero in the Royal blender, immediately there's an instinctive recoil. "Not for this," she seems to say. And so I stop whatever it is I'm doing and watch.

Arum Lilies

They arrive on Mother's Day. This is the only time of the year in which our house seems more like a garden center. I'm the only one who gives her books. I have two compelling reasons: first, variety is good; second, she grows anxious when dealing with the flowers. A couple of years back, Olive had a tall bush in her small garden that blocked my mother's view of the park. Ever since we got here, she's made it a routine to watch the flock of doves that gathers there. So, in a lamentably cruel and desperate attempt, she poured diesel on the bush. This sin has eaten at her to the point that it's become a curse. She believes that no plant will stay with her for long, no matter the care. I can't tell whether it's a self-fulfilling prophecy, yet it's true that plants abandon her rather quickly.

"My house is so beautiful every May. I wish it could last."

"It could, actually. Try something different this time."

"Oh, no, no. It's punishment. You know that."

"God helps those who help themselves, right?"

"I should have thought about that before losing it."

"Her garden's fine now. There's no use in resigning."

She sighs, as if my understanding were irredeemably earthbound. Nonetheless, she tends to them with love, and they stay with her for more than a week. I'm sure she wants to express her relief, her happiness, her surprise. But she keeps quiet, lest her presumptuous words snatch the life out of these lucent exceptions.

Homeopathic Pills

To her, it's common sense. If you have a degree, you're an expert. She's not dissuaded by the consequences of her idea. Astrology, sacred geometry, family constellations? Okay, so long as there's a university somewhere offering the degree. I don't mind her beliefs. What I do mind is her insistence on buying those pills for me. They're not particularly cheap and they're not particularly useful. Prudence. That's my one recurrent word to her.

"Under this roof, you're not doing whatever you like."

"But this is ridiculous. Why buy them for me? Go ahead, buy them for yourself. To me, they're just candy."

"I don't care. I'll make the believing for you."

"That money can help with the bills. Or anything else, to be honest."

"I'm doing very well, thank you. You're taking them."

"Oh for God's sake. It's the flu. That's it."

"The flu, the flu. I'm not stupid, not one bit. I've seen you all depressed and tetchy. Germán still asks about you. If only you stopped being so arrogant, he'd be someone you can lean on. I can't be everything in your life."

"Don't start. I appreciate his interest. He was very kind to me, but I can't do much more than send him my regards."

She's about to fly into one of her diatribes, but she takes a deep breath, slams on the table the small bottle labeled with my name, and goes to her room. The message is clear: be a man and throw it away.

Fat Buddha

It's on the bedside table, next to her otherwise Catholic assembly of saints. For years, she's sprinkled Buddhist paraphernalia around the house. All along I've followed with interest. In her heart of hearts, she must be an eclectic. And now, three weeks after the funeral of her sister-in-law, she's inclined to talk about metaphysics.

"I began sobbing when I was close to the casket. I felt possessed, I couldn't stop, I was crying with my whole body . . . you know how people say you can cry with your whole body? After a while, Melissa whispered that I was being overdramatic, that we had to leave."

"Amazing. What was it to her?"

"Maybe she was right. I don't know. It's just that . . . it took me by surprise. I thought we had said our goodbyes when she was in the hospital. I prayed, 'God, give me strength and let me leave her with a smile.' And it went as I had asked! I just didn't understand everything then."

"How do you feel right now?"

"Peaceful. But I have to confess that a thought crossed my mind as I was crying. It's probably true that there's no heaven. Just like your scientists say."

"Oh, don't start with that. You've said it yourself: they have no faith."

"And it looks like I'm not that far. I was in the house of our Lord!"

"I imagine . . . I mean, death is overwhelming to everyone. Those thoughts must cross every believer's mind."

"You know I read about a lot of religions. They're all so interesting. But they're also so varying. Why is mine the privileged one?"

"That's a question that drives many teenagers to atheism. And yet it's not so simple as that."

"Of course it isn't, of course. Here you have me, still praying in the morning for my family's health. But the

A Biography in Ten Objects

thought came so suddenly that I almost mistook it for a feeling."

"I bet it *was* a feeling."

"I was reading the *Bhagavad Gita* the other day and it seemed very silly. I couldn't shake the sensation. Then I wondered how people in India must feel when they read our Bible. They'd laugh, wouldn't they?"

"Why do Eastern religions interest you so much?"

"They offer some valuable lessons."

She does irradiate peace, even if it's woven with confusion and melancholy.

Bible

The first one she owned was very small and unbelievably robust. I hit it many, many times by accident, which filled me with guilt and inspired desperate rounds of prayer at night. Then, when we moved to the little apartment, she bought a new one that I can describe with only one word: august. She didn't get rid of the other. They had different functions. Robust for reading, august for garnishing. Yet we moved for a second time, and this was to be the bitter farewell of that small, stubborn companion. Though lost in a bus terminal, it would be heresy to deny the dignity of the occasion. I still maintain that as we were leaving California behind, I could distinguish from the bus's window a janitor who had it in his hands. The memory is not perfect: sometimes he is reading it while he eats chilaquiles from a topper, sometimes he has it in one hand while he carries a giant broom on the other. Either way, it found its place.

She always has it open in the Psalms. I've seen her read it—she's usually in the middle or toward the end. I once suspected she'd never read it through, especially because I couldn't remain awake in church when the priest recited passages. But she dispelled any doubts.

"I think it's time to read it from beginning to end. I did it when I was very young, so I can't say I remember much. I don't even know if I really got it. Probably not. I do remember it was violent . . . more than you'd expect."

"Why read it again?"

"To see if it turns out better."

She probably managed, but she never again touched on the attempt.

We're both reading in the living room now. I'm impressed to see that the baroque object in her hands has outlived—in more ways than one—maybe everything she's ever had. I have to ask. It's only natural.

"So, did you finish it?"

"I did! Took me the best of two years."

"Better?"

"With the exception of the violent parts, yes, it was better. There were things I still couldn't understand, but they somehow had an impact. Very strange, all of it."

"Ever reading it again?"

"No. I'm seventy years old. I expected to be dead by sixty-five. These remaining years are a gift, and gifts are supposed to be nice. I'll hold to the Psalms. Listen to this—*Deep calleth unto deep at the noise of thy waterspouts*: *all thy waves and thy billows are gone over me.* Difficult yet so beautiful-sounding."

I could censure the pessimistic undertones—I do, after all, wish her some kind of genuine immortality—but the enfolding zest is revealing and enough.

Draft

November, ———

DEAR RALI,
I remembered you this morning. I saw a little child playing marbles in the park. He was alone and severely concentrated, as if a false movement were to ruin something beyond the game. Children can be quite serious, perhaps more so than adults. Anyway, I found curious that he enjoyed such a dated pastime. He inspired me to write you a letter.

As you know, I have lived here in Guadalajara almost all my life. And you, well, you have lived across the whitewashed fence almost all your life. There is, however, an unfair advantage on my side: I've seen what your area looks like. So, in the spirit of a sterling judge, I will balance things out.

This city, like all cities in this wide continent, is pieced together haphazardly. The grand cathedrals are circled by ramshackle buildings and ailing stalls. The grand houses shed their ornaments and wait patiently for the vine's dalliance. Scraggy horses pull carriages filled with obese gentlemen. Every color that meets the eye is decaying, in imitation of the universal gray. Trash is sprinkled like a dash of cloves. Turgid projects parade their motley ruins. Nature is forced upon this mess in melancholy ways: through meager trees decorating median strips, through burnt-out hedges guarding abandoned sidewalks, through flowerpots impeding the flow of traffic.

There are those who find delight in this chaos. Or so they say. I think we have all grown accustomed. The city is not unlike a teenager's room: a permanent promise of order.

But enough of my incantatory descriptions. If I were to speak to you in person, I would use don Octavio's gruffer style: está pal perro. He is a good new friend of mine. An old-fashioned bitter wistful man. Which brings me to the people.

Young and old have few in common. That much is not surprising. Yet they share the oppression of nostalgia. Not in the usual sense, I must add. It is a very unearthly sort. One can catch a glimpse at the end of a night's heavy drinking. The eyelids struggle and a surge of hermetic sentences gathers in the air, leaving a dismal taste. I suspect the words come from the doorstep of sleep, where we are most like ourselves.

The presence of alcohol may make you skeptical of my point. Understandable. Humor offers alternative evidence. They cling to its cruelest slant. You know the one: that which happily disregards that truth is standing nearby. It is a carnival of degradation. You can see amid the confetti and belly-laughter an ideal that has been buried. I am unable to outline it. You must realize I am no keen psychologist. But maybe it would be an interesting exercise to find the true antonyms of their choice subjects: effeminacy, humility, ignorance, laziness. Do you not see in the horizon a rather conservative hero? I can hear the collective sigh.

Now, the act of generalization is a sad privilege. By snubbing the finer details, its broad brush tends toward bleak monotonous pictures. Oh, what horrors would I portray were I to tackle my native place! I am obligated to give you a miniature, then: the miniature of don Octavio.

He was born into a vast family, the youngest of seven boys and three girls. The father commanded an arduous respect. No one dared to stray from an earnest intonation when addressing him. But you will come to see that these authoritarian designs only reach the surface. Don Octavio relishes those nights in which he and his brothers, certain of their father's sleep and of the candle's life, dissected the paternal precepts and imagined their own. *You shall put your elbows on the table if you feel like it. You shall speak aloud if you can't contain your joy or anger. You shall work just in your free time. You shall feed the dogs more than twice a day if they wag their tails.* The mother, as is too often the case, was a pretty fountain into which everyone threw coins, almost demanding immediate wish-fulfillment. This was the solid and stubborn world that received my friend, and it is also the mirage that has kept him bitter and wistful. Adding a convenient lock, his father and his mother died young. Don Octavio sometimes says that they were in their forties, sometimes that they were in their thirties. It all depends on his intention to rhapsodize. They revealed to him a curse: not one member of the family had reached fifty. He grew without knowing how to treat his siblings. If he was too tender, his brothers reprimanded him (no seas joto/maricón/puñal). If he was too coarse, his sisters did (no seas cruel/cabrón/como ellos). He couldn't help it. He always thought about mornings the news would arrive. And the mornings came. All nine of them. Don Octavio is eighty-five years old, father of none. Why? He varies here, too. Sometimes the world is no place for children. Sometimes he wants to be the last flicker.

Sometimes his father talked with him in dreams and told him to live life on his own terms.

You may think there is an ironic touch in my retelling of don Octavio's years. It is not so. I have come to love him. He is an indisposed sage. You should see him rant about how life has only taught him two miserable things: that one head is better than a thousand and that a thousand hands are better than two. Peculiar inclination for numbers and paradoxes, wouldn't you agree?

Before I close, I'll tell you a story about your mother. It fits nicely in this whole rendering of the details.

When she was eight, she worked with me on the orange juice stand. You've heard of it. We were first-rate in a space that had no shortage of rambunctious sellers. Better yet, we were straightforward: one manual juicer, one pitcher with a colander, one pack of plastic cups, one knife, and a pile of oranges. Your mother took care of the money. Near us, there was a peanut vendor: another woman with a little boy. He did the hard work. But children couldn't care less about things in common. He and your mother quickly became friends. And the activity that most filled their hearts was feeding the great pariah of the street: a grimy crippled Labrador. They were very perceptive: they fed it in secret. They had already seen how its hunger roused everyone's ire. The dog learned to meet them in a deserted corner. It had once tried to approach our stands, perhaps expecting a difference, but the little boy's mother chased it off with a small wooden shovel. I can still recall their swelling pockets. Your mother had a beautiful red dress with two of them. The little boy had blue worn-out trousers with four of them. I managed to help out from time to time. It was important to me, however, that they didn't notice. This was their initiative. It ended when the tired Labrador growled at them and tried biting the little boy. Without delay, one of the vendors was dragging it to its execution. I imagine the commotion muffled the dog's cries. I can only remember afterward its rigid body thrown into a garbage bag. It is a black memory, yet one that carries a consoling companion: your mother and the little boy undaunted, insisting on cramming their pockets the very next day.

Rereading this letter, I see that my original purpose was an excuse. I am grateful for it. I must leave now.

Lovingly,

L.

Alive and Well

I

THEY INSISTED on telling her to smile, on gathering proof of her contentment with life. But the resigned compliance was her way of asking to be left alone. When the photo session was finished, she suddenly wasn't of any interest to them; she was then little more than a sick old woman they had to take care of in order to get some government aid.

My aunt and uncle were normal people, with all the traditional shortcomings this description implies. Aunt Rose was short, spherical, and severe-looking. She had been married to a man named Santiago. Nobody in the family could give an adequate account of their ephemeral marriage; much of this had to do with his protracted absences, which were explained through domestic mythmaking—he was a remarkable coyote, a drug dealer, and a wandering priest. They had a son, Ian, who was twelve years old by the time they divorced. Aunt Rose vehemently avoided the topic of Santiago; she didn't hesitate when a slap was needed. My aunts said he was the only man she had ever been with.

Uncle Enrique was short, spherical, and pasty. He had been married fifteen years to Veronica, a religious fanatic with a withered face who everyone suspected had looked like that since birth. She dictated the days he could see us and for how long, and this extended to all his activities—a mild stutter marked his attempts to doubt, but she had a cultivated rage. This was Veronica's defining trait: she would lash out against anybody at any moment. Everyone liked to remember the night she theatrically spit out the Cajun chicken pasta, a dish Aunt Mary had just learned to prepare, because it had too much salt; she screamed at Uncle Enrique and later at Aunt Mary for not considering her diet. "That woman. No respect for anyone. None." Those were the words Aunt Carmen used to chastise Uncle Enrique every time she saw him. Whenever Uncle Ray was drunk, he called Uncle Enrique a sissy and gave him a lecture on what were the defining traits of a man. Once, Uncle Enrique did his best to counter this by pointing out that at least he could keep a woman for over a year. "You're not keeping her; she's keeping you," Uncle Ray answered, with a fake but contagious laughter that made light of what would be Uncle Enrique's only attempt to defend himself. Veronica had made him wait five years to have a son; her excuses involved convoluted theological speculation. His name was Daniel. He had a prodigious memory. Veronica repeatedly asked him to recite whole chapters from Ecclesiastes at family reunions. It was an odd spectacle, and my aunts didn't find it particularly admirable, but they obliged so as to avoid tensions with Uncle Enrique. I suspected the boy had no understanding of what he was saying because even I had to struggle to find meaning to the words. Uncle Ray asked Veronica about this at some point; her answer was a prolonged grimace. Afterward, addressing no one in particular, she said, "He understands what he says. Enrique and I talk to him about every single word." Uncle Enrique was worried that Daniel didn't show warmth toward us. "He isn't like this with Veronica's relatives. He's a tender kid. Maybe he's just shy; he spends more time with them," he would say to us. But it had already been years.

Uncle Enrique crumbled the day he revealed the divorce to the family. Two years had passed since Aunt Rose's, an unsavory fact, for he had had the conviction that time made marriages sturdy: he believed in epoch-making problems that kept things fresh. Everyone asked him about his role in the debacle, but he refused to give details. A month later, he lost his job and began living with Aunt Carmen, who had always felt very close to him. She cooked for him and, with the reluctant help of Aunt Mary, handed him money to get by.

Aunt Carmen never married; she said she preferred using those energies to help out the people closest to her. She was the only one of my aunts who had many friends outside the family, some of whom were former lovers who had gone on to have families of their own. Such was her altruism that I felt cynical trying to pinpoint its limits (a disreputable exercise in any context, some may say, although one that I find useful when it comes to identifying hypocrisy, as was the case with Veronica, who seldom failed to preach the doctrine of love, even if she herself could bestow it only after careful calculations not unlike those of a stockbroker, or as was the case with Uncle Enrique, why not say it, who liked to think himself a magnanimous brother, husband, and father, all three roles at which he failed to the point of not being worthy of the two most condescending words of our language: *nice try*). But, as I said, no one like Uncle Enrique. My mother gathered this was because of their age. They were the oldest siblings. At the time of the divorce, Uncle Enrique was fifty years old; Aunt Carmen, forty-eight; Aunt Mary, forty-three; Uncle Ray, forty; Aunt Rose, thirty-eight; and my mother, thirty-three. This list clearly disproved her hypothesis. Aunt Mary and Uncle Ray weren't close. Neither were Aunt Rose and my mother.

Uncle Enrique approached me one day at a family dinner while everyone else was still at the table. He had excused himself to go to the bathroom. He thought I didn't have any preconceptions about him; at least not about his life decisions. What could a high-school kid think about them?

"Did you know your grandma had another stroke recently?"

"Yeah, Mom told me. I haven't been to the hospital."

"It was very serious. She will need to be cared for consistently."

"Mom talked about a nursing home."

"What! Nonsense. She has sons! We love her and wouldn't let her be treated like an object. I've talked about this with Rose. We will take care of anything she needs. Nobody will have to worry too much about her well-being except us."

"Oh. That's good. You'll live with her?"

"Yes, we have to. This will also benefit the family, make it more united. Rose has been very lonely since she divorced and hasn't had much contact with your grandma, or with your other aunts. She'll leave the house to Ian."

He was careful not to talk about his situation: he had been searching for a job and a place to live. At Aunt Carmen's house, the place for weekly reunions, he announced the decision to take complete care of my grandmother to the rest of the family. Uncle Ray was indignant and supported my mother's idea. As usual, he was drunk.

"You fucking slimy opportunist. Do you have any idea how to care for the elderly? Are you a damn nurse? Let me see your credentials. You weren't there the first time. I can't believe how much of a fucking coward you are. And to think you're dragging poor Rose into your shit. Take responsibility for once, you sad excuse of a man. My mother needs a professional to take care of her full-time. There's no going around it. You're not going to use her to rebuild your fucking life. You ruined it; you fix it. Leave my mother out! Rose, take care of your son instead."

My aunts tried to calm him, but this awakened his dramatic instincts. He stormed out of the house. Uncle Enrique was bright red and shaking. When Aunt Carmen tried to comfort him, he started sobbing. Aunt Rose was as unfazed as Aunt Mary and my mother.

The event split the family in two: Uncle Ray and my mother distanced themselves abruptly. Since then, my mother called Aunt Carmen just to know my grandmother's condition.

II

When I was nine years old, I was close to my grandmother. She did all that was in her hands to distract me from my mother's situation back then. This involved actually playing with my toys, having conversations about cartoons, and a number of other activities that adults commonly avoid so as not to lose authority. I was under the impression that she existed exclusively to dedicate her energies to me. In a sense, this was true: she was unfriendly to everyone who wasn't my mother and me.

The majority of her neighbors were openly hostile to her. I would catch their face contortions and eye-rolls. She gave no importance to this. I never heard a word from her about the neighbors, not even about Harvey, the one person on the block who persisted in being friendly to her. He would shower her with good mornings, good afternoons, and good nights, but got back only reluctant hellos. I liked him. I found it admirable that he wore a suit; nobody else I knew did. It was an old-fashioned gray check three-piece suit. Not a day passed in which it didn't seem lustrous. More admirable was that, like my grandmother, he apparently didn't work. Same spot, same people. A marvelous hassle—sharpness for sharpness' sake. However, none of this was of concern to my grandmother. Her world was much too narrow to include suit-wearing gentlemen, and, let me insist, I was glad.

Aunt Mary's visits were the only frequent ones in those days—the best of her life; you had to look at her face when she recalled them. She worked as a sous chef in a decent restaurant three blocks from my grandmother's house. She had started out as a prep cook and was able to climb the ladder in a year. A natural. Her talks with my grandmother involved tirades against the head chef and long anecdotes that would form the core of all her future conversations. Sometimes my grandmother asked Aunt Mary about her marriage prospects; she was "already" thirty-seven. The usual answer: she was comfortable with not being married; her ten-year relationship was "healthy enough not to require defibrillation."

Uncle Enrique and Uncle Ray were especially absent. Everyone knew the reasons: Veronica in the case of the former, and alcohol in the case of the latter. My grandmother was a virtuoso of resentment. Whenever they visited, subtle manipulations of face muscles near her jaw brimmed with accusations. Uncle Enrique couldn't handle the pressure and readily made excuses for his absence, all of which avoided the subject of Veronica. Uncle Ray went on with the formalities of the occasion.

Eventually, I was as absent as my uncles. I retained some affection for my grandmother, but I couldn't help finding the rare visit a chore. There were no toys or cartoons left for her to connect in any way with me as I grew older. Our time spent together changed. I played the role of noisemaker so she could feel someone was around the house. It didn't go beyond rustling the dishes on my trips to the kitchen.

Uncle Ray was visiting when she had her first stroke. I was fourteen years old then. He told us in the hospital how it all happened: the left side of her face drooped and she started to slur a name constantly—Fernando. It proved an obstacle when speaking to her. Our exchange at the hospital was brief and somewhat bitter.

"Grandma. It's me, Omar."
"Fernando?"
"Omar, Grandma, your grandson."
"Tell them to get inside already."
"What? My aunts? I think they already saw you."
"The rascals. Get them in!"
"Grandma?"

She smiled. The smile was completely mechanical, purified from any intention. Her eyes were fixed on a scenery that was not available to anyone but her. I'm sure she didn't recognize me. She held the smile an unnatural amount of time and then, without a change in her eyes, let her lips rest in a perfectly horizontal position, one usually reserved for photo IDs. I caressed her hand and left.

There were talks about recovery. She would have a part-time nurse, and my aunts and uncles would alternate taking care of her. Like all plans, it was modified while being applied. Aunt Carmen and my mother went from Monday to Friday. The others fought to see who would go on weekends. I remember asking Aunt Carmen whether she was upset; I knew my mother was.

"I understand. They have families."

"But they were all terribly worried about her when she was at the hospital."

"And I'm sure they were sincere. The thing is, people can't retain the intensity of a feeling for too long; it would drive them crazy. They have to focus on their daily trifles. I believe that's where everyone's energies should be. They can be the worst of nightmares if left unchecked."

"What about you?"

"Friends normally don't need any attentions. And my mother does now. I can give them to her without compromise."

I couldn't avoid thinking about an uncomfortable truth that was lurking in the background: they saw my grandmother as I did before the stroke. Yet it was difficult to condemn anyone. Her identity wasn't cohesive; her sense of time was ravished. The word *burden* loomed through everyone's mind. And how could it not? My grandmother was at the threshold of impersonality.

Uncle Enrique's divorce and the second stroke came in less than a year.

III

"I remember Fernando. He wasn't much of a dad, really. Carmen would agree. Your grandma had a difficult time with him. He was allergic to staying at home with us."

"Did my other aunts and uncle know him?"

"No. They had an actual dad—Gustavo."

"Are there any photos?"

"Your grandma had one with Fernando, but she burned it after he left. I don't know why she didn't have one with Gustavo. Maybe she wasn't as close to him."

An average conversation with Uncle Enrique when I visited. He had left most of the family vexed after his decision to take care of my grandmother, and in me he found a redeeming figure. He emphasized his childhood, finding in it multiple instances of neglect that justified the way he had led his life: no affection, no caring father, no education. I couldn't tell whether he believed any of this; Aunt Carmen did well under similar circumstances. Nevertheless, I was not interested in the role. During the first two years, I visited once a week because my mother grew skeptical of Aunt Carmen and could visit only once a month. I wasn't there voluntarily.

Aunt Rose and I didn't talk; she limited herself to nods and monosyllables. Her severe expression had melted away the unique features of her face, and it sometimes amazed me to find her breathing; she could construct coherent sentences—all she had left to be distinguished from my grandmother. Time has a tendency to solidify strain.

There was a contrast in the way Aunt Rose and Uncle Enrique handled their responsibilities. However, it was superficial. Uncle Enrique exuded enthusiasm when attending my grandmother; he talked to her as if she were a newborn. Yet whenever he lifted her from the couch, you could see in his grip certain desperation and aggressiveness—think about the grip preceding a spontaneous threat. Unlike him, Aunt Rose showed no interest in pretending; she was rather cynical.

My visits didn't overlap with those of Aunt Mary and Aunt Carmen. Uncle Enrique told me they visited once every two or three weeks and helped around the house. A sense of dread overran me when I realized how much time my grandmother actually spent with Aunt Rose and Uncle Enrique. I worried that she would lose her ability to speak. The second stroke left her with a mixture of smiles, nods, and the sound of her mouth opening midway as a means of communication. My aunt and uncle weren't helping. They didn't even demand these signs from her. Instead of asking about her preferred food, they would give her whatever they were eating. Instead of asking about her favorite channel, they would put on whatever pleased them. My uncle's babbling was just that, babbling; it didn't require any response, and it made more conspicuous the sad analogy—my grandmother was like an infant, a neglected infant who didn't have enough time left to learn the basics of language on her own. My complete affection for her was back, and I felt guilty of retrieving it under these pathetic circumstances. But I was also relieved because she couldn't be considered a burden anymore: there was a person in front of everyone's eyes; words were not able to betray her.

The weekly visits stopped once Aunt Rose and Uncle Enrique got a grasp of social media. I then visited once a month or every two months. This made visits more bearable because I would get to see Aunt Mary, Aunt

Carmen, and even Harvey, who sometimes sat on the veranda of his modest house. His good afternoons and good nights were warm and gave continuity to things long disjointed. What I found irritating, however, was that Aunt Rose and Uncle Enrique talked to him; I couldn't help thinking this was part of Uncle Enrique's act. He was fooling around with the pillar of those memories I shared with my grandmother. When I didn't see anyone other than Aunt Rose and Uncle Enrique during my visits, I stayed for two hours at most. Sufficient time to see the daily ritual of making my grandmother pose for the family. Uncle Enrique had been aware for a while that I was no redeemer; I suppose he sought validation elsewhere. He waited for the day someone would tell him, "You've earned that money. You're not an opportunist. You've done what you could with your life."

IV

My mother contacted Uncle Ray when Ian and Daniel went to live with my grandmother. She lived in a small three-bedroom house; an emaciated figure on the couch came immediately to mind. The second stroke was now four years away. I had stopped visiting a year earlier, but my mother continued her monthly visits. Uncle Ray and my mother agreed they would take my grandmother to a nursing home at last. Improvisation at its finest.

The sight of Uncle Ray was baffling. Time had given him a beating as severe as the one Aunt Rose had received, if not worse. His body was not made to withstand alcohol and loneliness. In the four years I hadn't seen him, he had lost his jocose, manly demeanor. Everything straight in him had gone crooked.

Resentment had given up its shock absorbers. As far as I knew, my mother was the only one who had kept in touch with him.

Although the plan was improvised, it wasn't executed hastily. Uncle Ray stayed with us for a week. My mother wanted to make clear to him he wasn't there just to fix things. She also took care he didn't drink while visiting. Soon enough he asked me about Aunt Rose and Uncle Enrique.

"How is he doing?"

"I haven't visited in a while."

"When you last saw him."

"He managed."

"He managed . . . a good way to manage, a good way to manage. How did Rose do?"

"She seemed sullen."

"I don't know that word, boy."

"Unhappy, tired."

"She better be. That's the least she could do. A little bit of guilt. To leave your son alone to go beg the government for money. Here you have it: the kid's back. But Enrique manages. What a surprise! When has he ever had to face up to things? He manages and he invites his son to the *party*."

I didn't have an answer to that compressed diatribe, not even a polite one. This had always been Uncle Ray's specialty: cornering people. His eyes wouldn't leave room for relaxing; they chased after you. But he changed the subject after letting hang the clunky last word of his speech, as if realizing it had diminished the seriousness and impact he was aiming for.

On our way to my grandmother's house, nobody spoke in the car. Uncle Ray had a clenched fist on the dashboard. I didn't take this lightly. Was he eager to beat up Uncle Enrique? Violence was unnecessary—

Uncle Enrique had enough with being himself. Perhaps I was reading too much into it, but when we arrived Uncle Ray dashed out of the car. My mother rushed after him.

"Ray! Ray! Wait! Come over here. Don't be dramatic."

"Dramatic?"

"Yes. You're sober. Act like it. Okay?"

Uncle Ray stared at my mother and waited for her to knock on the door. Uncle Enrique opened. He tried to smile and say something, but Uncle Ray and my mother entered as if he weren't there. My grandmother was on the couch next to Aunt Rose. They were watching television. My mother hesitated before explaining the reason for the unexpected visit; she wasn't sure whom to address. She glanced at Uncle Ray, who seemed to be studying the house. Uncle Enrique was waiting for her to speak; he got the message that they were not in the mood for conventional preludes.

"Enrique, we came to talk to my mother."

"*Our* mother."

"You understand perfectly well what I mean."

"It sounds divisive."

"Our mother. We came to talk to our mother."

"Ray, I . . . how are you? I haven't known from you in a while. It's . . . well, strange. Oh, and Omar. You've also been lost. Would any of you want a glass of water, some tea . . . ?"

"Thanks, Enrique, we're fine. We're taking my mother to a nursing home."

Before Uncle Enrique could revise my mother's use of the possessive, Aunt Rose got off the couch and raised her voice.

"Again? We talked about this years ago. She's doing okay with us. Stop this already!"

"Rose, I thought the same thing. But she's weaker than ever, and she really needs a professional. We should all agree on this."

"A professional. Ha! She has us."

Uncle Ray rubbed his face and went to sit next to my grandmother. He took her hand. She smiled the usual mechanical smile and didn't turn to look at him. My mother kept arguing with Aunt Rose. Nobody had lost his composure. The subject of Ian and Daniel hadn't been brought up. They weren't in the house.

"You can't take her! She won't want to go. She likes being in her house. Who would want to be kicked out of his house?"

"She would have wanted it."

"You barely come and visit her! You don't know what she wants. We live with her."

"I've lived with her many times in my life. I'm sure I understand my own mother's wishes."

"So do we."

"I know. That's why we should reach an agreement, something that will benefit her the most. Let's not think about us."

Uncle Ray had his face covered with one hand while still holding that of my grandmother. The air was getting heavy. I knew the exchange would escalate. I find it strange that people expect reason to play a major role when it comes to family discussions. Nothing related to family is rational. It's despotically governed by the unconscious and the irrational. But here was my mother doing her best to appear a reasonable person, a facade Aunt Rose and Uncle Enrique found unbearable. Reason sounds patronizing to the unreasonable, more so when it's something that's trying to pass for it—a mellow voice, for example.

"Go ahead. Ask her."

Alive and Well

My mother went over to my grandmother. I walked out of the house and sat on the steps of the porch. It was an expansive day. Harvey enjoyed it sitting on his veranda with a brand new suit, or at least one I hadn't seen before. He hadn't noticed me, and things were better that way. I didn't want to ruin his solitude, a solitude as expansive as the day, and perhaps as vital. How could there exist such a startling contrast between my grandmother and him? Family was a tempting answer. He was no family man. I never saw him with company. For an instant, I felt bitter. I was raised to think of myself as someone who had to stay close to his kin. There was no way around it. I didn't have solitude as an alternative, just loneliness.

Uncle Ray and my mother came outside and hurried to the car. They didn't turn around to look at me. I stood up and stepped into the house. My grandmother was asleep. Aunt Rose and Uncle Enrique sat next to her. I sat across them in the old single sofa chair. They were watching an infomercial. We didn't talk about what happened. We didn't talk. They fell asleep. I went to my grandmother's bedroom for a blanket and covered them with it. Outside, Harvey was dozing off. Uncle Ray and my mother had left. They would keep trying.

In her inertial and childish way, my grandmother played the perennial role of a thread to which everybody hung on.

A Threefold Cord

As I help Fátima's father carry the flowers, he complains about his back.

"A bunch of delicate things putting me to the test. Can you believe it?"

I'm close to laughing, but I do my best to keep it a smile when we near the entrance. Most of Fátima's cousins are gathered round a coffee-filled table. The disposable cups seem untouched. You can still see the vapor rising from them; on the whole, you wouldn't suspect they were theirs. Some of her cousins browse their phones, others whisper and signal a grin. Those who see us wave aloofly. We leave the flowers next to others' arrangements.

Fátima's mother approaches with heavy steps. Everyone's apathetic mood gives way to a measure of solemnity. They lock their phones and hide them, hush, stand straight, smooth out their shirt. One by one, they hug her. They all seem unsure whether to speak. Perhaps they sense that by doing so, they'll undermine her frail silence. Her eyes rarely fasten on theirs. She stares into the distance. The moment she leaves, they resume the manner in which they intend to spend the night.

I haven't exchanged a word with Fátima. She's concentrated on her mother. Aside from helping with the flowers, I'm at a loss. Her father seems as disoriented as I am. We follow them into the main room. It is slightly empty. There is a large, pristine table in the center, on which a spare plate of cookies rests. Only one of Fátima's uncles, the youngest, is sitting here with his family. He embraces his sister, who at last is in no hurry. She breaks down. He remains calm and greets us with a nod. Fátima is touched by this gesture and rushes toward one of the bathrooms.

I sit in a chair nearby. The door to the chapel is in front of me. I can distinguish the rest of the uncles and aunts. Unlike the youngest, they look overwhelmed. As much as I would like to offer my condolences now, I somehow feel alien to the whole situation and thus fear they might suspect insincerity. I wait for Fátima's lead. Her parents, meanwhile, enter without us. There is immediate commotion.

Fátima trudges to the chapel's door. She pauses and glances in my direction, then lowers her head and goes inside. I catch up. The casket hasn't been brought. I try not to prolong my interactions, expecting a laconic demeanor to compel everyone to forget me. Nevertheless, one of her uncles grips my hand with both of his. He does so almost desperately.

"It means very much to me that you're here. Very much."

I grab his shoulder and give a weary smile. Fátima, with swollen eyes, asks whether I would like some coffee. Before I answer, she hands me a cup. It is only now that I notice everyone here has one pressed against their chest. A gradual silence harmonizes the varying degrees of grief. Fátima and I head to the main room.

"They're tired. They're at that point in which you just can't keep crying."

"I know."

The families are slow to arrive. Their dispersal is uniform: the young ones to the lobby, the middle-aged to the main room—the lone close relative to the chapel. The large, pristine table gluts with plates and used napkins. People begin talking after a respectable number of minutes. One would figure a single subject, but no: love, maturity, parenthood, genetics, family values, loans, crime rates, vagrancy, rehabilitation, God are all discussed. I believe a conjectural biographer could glean an authentic portrait from the variations upon these seemingly disparate themes; with no more than an ear to listen, of course.

Fátima props her head on one of her hands and makes an effort to stay awake. In front of us, her youngest uncle plays with his daughter and answers his wife, who is sketching anecdotes to her sisters, whenever she needs to recall a detail.

"Have you spoken with Adrian?"

"No. We said hello. That's it."

"What about your uncle's sons?"

"I gave my condolences."

"They looked okay, don't you think?"

"Yes."

In every remark I am torn between dismal comfort and genuine doubt. Although I'm aware that in these moments it is best to be quiet, I'm confronted again with the matter of perceived insincerity.

I go out for air. Adrian, Fátima's most opinionated yet beloved cousin, breaks off his conversation to approach me.

"A cigarette would be nice, wouldn't it?"

"Couldn't agree more."

"But, you know, it's not an option. They still see us as kids."

"Guess that wouldn't apply to me."

"Ha. They've already made their mind up about you. It wouldn't mesh."

"No cigarettes, then."

"My uncle liked them. For a while he hid the habit, but . . . things didn't work out with Aunt Flor, and that was that."

"Can't blame him."

"He fucked up his life, though. I know Fátima hates to hear it, but it's true."

"It's difficult to talk about it. That's for sure. He is, in the end, her uncle. Was."

"It's fine. He *is* our uncle."

"And he was good to her."

"I'm not disagreeing with that. I'm talking about his life as a whole. There's Aunt Flor, Leobardo, Elena . . ."

"I get it. But there's also many other people. How would you even begin to calculate all of that?"

"Ask around one day."

"It will be a mix. It's always a mix."

He appears to meditate his answer; a hearse then parks close to us. I pat Adrian's back and hurry inside. As the realization that the casket has arrived furthers, body after body tenses. Fátima is no longer in the main room. I intend to look for her in the chapel, but I'm struck by the sight of her youngest uncle—he is sitting still, with both hands clasped near his face, almost as in prayer; the sonorous approach of the casket seems to increase the speed at which his left leg fidgets. His wife and her sisters are distracted by the murmurs and stand as soon as the casket enters. He remains concentrated elsewhere. The casket is slowly moved toward the chapel. There is a minor struggle to position it in proper relation to the door. In the midst of this, he reaches for one of the casket's edges and taps it. He gets up, adjusts his belt, and follows the casket through the door. Coughs mingle with wails.

Eventually, the tension subsides. Now, however, the conversations steer along obscure routes. They are far more idiosyncratic—intimate, even. I distract myself by looking at the corporate-like minimalism of the funeral home. It is amusing to find how much it contributes to the general solemnity—with acoustics that propel the faintest step into shrieks, with barren colors that pummel any mirth, with apathetic employees who hint at a residue of sympathy. You must be reminded of the proper etiquette: affliction or shame.

I am handed over a half-full cup of coffee.

"Can I lie down and push my feet against you?"

"Sure, sure. Go ahead."

She is done. I am done. Most are done.

I look forward to the burial, where the off-key guitar and humble snare drum will play old songs that'll excuse the breach of manners.

As the Waters Fail from the Sea

THERE IS NO GREAT DIFFICULTY in keeping books free from dust. My father knows this better than I do. You just need a brush and some patience. But you would not suspect it by looking at his bookstore; you would imagine that there must exist an abstruse method available exclusively to the rare book and manuscript libraries of the world.

We've discussed the matter, and he obstinately clings to an eccentric aesthetic theory (one of many), in which the categories of beauty and ugliness are substituted with those of old and new. Even if I believe it to be destitute of weight, similar to untold other caprices born from the minds of cranks, it has its charm. The exposition came when I first began helping him out.

"Why do you let so much dust gather?"

"It becomes books."

"What?"

"It is their baptism. A memento of their endurance and hope. They are no longer an idea, an idle lightning, but the solid incursion of soul."

"That seems quite the high-flown rationalization of laziness."

"Let me use your irony to exemplify a larger meaning. Irony is the province of youth—of the new; sincerity, the province of age—of the old. One cannot bother finding its way out of self-imposed urbanity; the other moves and takes pride in its vigor. One corrodes; the other galvanizes. And so it is with all: polish and dust, reason and emotion, thought and action."

While the theory itself lacks consistency, it is not so with my father's devotion to it. He is scrupulous. All the bookshelves are made of English oak, and most are Victorian—a pattern that reigns over the rest of the furniture. Perhaps half of his earnings have gone into the practice of his theory. A small space, therefore, is natural. Yet I am sometimes impressed by my father's craft. When you enter the bookstore, you are reminded of Rembrandt's sparse luxuriance. And within you can almost feel a glimmer of reverence. Obstinacy is old, he would say.

Used books are a declining commodity. Hence, the customers are easily typecast. The great majority arises from the ashes of would-be sellers, people who believe buying a book beforehand might help their case. But it is habitually a lost one: here they come, with a truckful of inherited encyclopedias, assuming that even if they find them useless, there must be others who will rejoice. "One man's trash is another man's treasure." A tacit adage that, as all the rest, does not quite fit reality. It is my duty to disappoint them. I had a hard time before I settled into my father's curt words. I would try consolation, advice, small talk. It meant little. "No one is buying; better to donate." The only sellers we are really interested in are the deserters, people who once thought philosophy or literature would make their lives soar into the metaphysical realm, failing to understand it was all a teenage romance. My father has bought from them first-rate volumes: Traill's *The Works of Thomas Carlyle*, Waller & Glover's *The Collected Works of William Hazlitt*, Richard de Bury's *Philobiblon*. Though he says they will do the store good, I glean from the assigned prices there is no real interest in parting with them. Moreover, he reserves for them a neoclassical glass-door bookcase. I have long thought of it as his canon. How could it not be? It permeates his whole life: his manners, his diction, his motions, his temperament. You can see Carlyle and Hazlitt in his incoherent passion, Johnson and Tolstoy in his zealous earnestness, Emerson and Melville in his prolix mysticism, James and Hume in his pluralistic view of the universe, de Bury in his handling of books. We also have the vagrant parents, who notice a bookshelf and presume its contents the Library of Babel. They can be insistent but lose heart with ease whenever you explain the nature of the finite. A radical departure from those who come looking for popular books. The most stubborn of all, they must be treated furtively, since my father makes it a duty to heap scorn on them. Once more, the consistency in act is praiseworthy, though I cringe at his self-righteous harangues. Accordingly, as the years go by, fewer and fewer casual readers dare tread this inauspicious corner. The privilege, if you feel in the elitist mood, goes to the great minority, composed of people as sour and idiosyncratic as my father. They roam the bookstore for hours, turn the dust into creases, and absent-mindedly listen to him, who becomes expansive in their vicinity. Indeed, there is something cheerless about the affair: this reserved old man, as a rule tight-lipped, judges these instants adequate to bare his soul. The one reason I have refrained from intervening is that he somehow ascends then. With the scraps he receives as answers he constructs evanescent cenotaphs to his heroes. He seems awake.

Thus it is that in a very real sense my father is alone. He has driven my mother away through his unremitting criticisms, which suggest he hoped for a sparring partner. He has driven me away through his sealed deportment, which suggests he hoped for a *locum tenens*. I have dreamt that the bookstore burns and he escapes, suddenly in the clutches of an epiphany: it all builds up to a barrier, nothing else. He knows where I stand—I will not carry the torch. Nor do I believe others will. He knows this. And a decision seems to have been reached.

Opening the front door has grown difficult. A pile of books that months ago made no difference now accounts for the blockage. My father, characteristically, has little to say. "Leave them alone." It may be an aesthetic choice, another brush-stroke that adds a strange distinction, akin to the sky's borders in Rembrandt's *Mill*. It may be a form of study that facilitates his wild flights. Or perhaps it is an inconvenience born from necessity. Or even a promise of change. I am inclined to maintain a bracing tide of speculations, but I must resist, for the truth is there, pristine and unapologetic: the door will cease to open; the tomb is finished.

Antisophers

I

ALTHOUGH LONG DISTANCED from the academic clique, Faustino and Dayana were widely known within our university. It struck me as odd at first—here were two very distinct persons, whose lives were not parallel or easily recounted as dedicated to one great endeavor. They were not the sort of figures who found a comfortable place in memory. Dayana had been a hectic activist for most of her life: few were the causes she didn't have the heart and energy to support; she was an impressive counterexample to the majority of our professors, who once espoused hopes of social betterment and later "came to their senses." Her name was met either with a condescending smile or a moderate scoff. Faustino, on the other hand, had given his life to writing books and "publishing" them by independent means; he was also a counterexample, for his prose was incandescent and his thoughts foreign to the self-important, minute, jargon-laden articles we were assigned to read. His name elicited a somewhat more sympathetic response, since he led as sedentary an existence as any tenured professor—no tip of the hat, however.

Understandably, then, Emily and I were intrigued by the prospect of an interview. Faustino had just written *The Imaginative Leap*, and Dayana was rumored to have started her memoirs. Moreover, the first issue of our fledgling magazine had not been stillborn; we managed to sell a bit more than half of the printings. It seemed things were in place. So we asked Krumrie, our Logic professor, to help with the arrangements. He was an old friend of theirs, one of the few left in the university. Given his discreet nature, you had to ask about the friendship to get any details, and even then he was quite laconic.

"I first made the acquaintance of Dayana. She wasn't as certain of things back then as she is now. She appreciated discussion. I remember how after every single class she did not seem convinced of the arguments. 'Ad hoc, is what that was.'"

"When did she begin worrying about social matters?"

"I'm not sure. She was skeptical of Marx and the Frankfurt School, curiously. The normal gateways, no?"

"What about Faustino?"

"I got to know him about a year later. Impatient, fickle. He hasn't changed much. He berated the need for formalizations in some classes. 'I've had it with these onanistic intellectual games.'"

If pressed further, he doubled down on his uncertainty; trying with the present had similar results. The two phrases he quoted were his lone contribution, always repeated when recalling the couple's youth. He may have thought they summed them up.

Emily and I didn't speculate about his possible reaction to our asking for help contacting his old friends, so it took us aback.

"An interview? The university is teeming with rigorous thinkers and activists who are already dealing with obscurity. I'm not sure Dayana and Faustino would be of much help."

"We understand, but they could offer an outside perspective. Life here can be too insular at times."

"It is precisely that insularity which sharpens focus. Students are fuzzy reasoners as things stand. Dayana and Faustino tempt them into an idiosyncratic lifestyle. I fear it is difficult for the average student to ponder this properly."

While I searched for a diplomatic answer, Emily went forth.

"You're talking as a stuffy teacher, Krumrie. And that's fine. But we would like to give him a choice."

"I will talk to them. Do not be readily swayed. Maintain your independence."

It was puzzling to know Krumrie was a close friend. We were familiar with his orthodox ways and impeccable academic record, but there had been elbow room for rationalizations—he opened up with them, he lived vicariously through their insurgency, he held in high regard the old days, etc. Not anymore. His manner was brusque, as if an esoteric principle had been forced to fracture. Yet Emily and I were pleased enough.

The interview was set for a Saturday afternoon. Friday night, Emily complained about the questions we'd written down.

"This is so lifeless. They're the type of questions we'd throw at Krumrie, you know."

"I admit they're not original or whatever, but we can't just chat for a while. The activism and the writing belong to the foreground. Besides, we don't have any idea about the kind of people they are. They might be curmudgeons."

"Yeah, we're not a gossip magazine—not yet, at least. But we can come up with something more natural."

"As long as we plan ahead, you won't be seeing anything natural."

"You're right. Here's my idea: let's make an outline, let's leave behind the specific words. It'll be something of an improvisation."

"Just don't die on me."

II

Their house was on the outskirts of the city. Though modest, it stood as a heavy contrast to those in the surroundings. To begin with, it wasn't mired in dirt, it didn't amass a blend of bricks and mortar that sullied hanging laundry in the front yard, it didn't have a fence made of alternating pieces of cardboard and wood—all in all, it was an actual home. And this sight strained our already shaky morale. As we waited outside, their neighbors stared and whispered.

Faustino was the first to greet us. He waved at the neighbors and cracked some local joke. Predictably unkempt, he nonetheless seemed in high spirits.

"Was it a bother getting here?"

"Not at all."

"He's being nice. You live . . . very, very far away from uni. Deliberate?"

"Somewhat. Matters of money that ended up acquiring nifty symbolic value."

I could notice the tension between Emily's blunt words and the hesitant tone, but Faustino didn't flinch. I was moderately relieved.

The interior was something of a mismatch: a long bookcase that seemed to spill miscellaneous objects over the floor (magazines, newspapers, notebooks, pencils, markers) covered most of the living room wall; in the remaining space, impeccable, a tall, elongated pot bore the weight of two hyacinths. Dayana, who sat on a worn-out couch nearby, accentuated the disparity. She wore a black dress that served as canvas to her ashen hair.

"Oh, are you Krumrie's students? I wasn't expecting such youth!"

Her transition from seriousness to levity was sudden yet natural. Soon we felt comfortable enough to begin recording. Emily would have the lead for a while before handing over the notebook.

"For a long time both of you have had an increasingly sterling reputation among young students. Do you find this understandable or rather strange?"

"It's not too surprising. Day and I have done our best to maintain the energy and hopes of bygone years. Some of that must come through."

"It's always heartwarming to know sincere work can inspire others. However, I *do* find it strange. Take a look at history's regal pile of books and events—hardly anyone feels its pulse. Few things seize the minds of twenty-year-olds."

"We have the supreme advantage of being alive, Day."

"Most of our friends appreciate your status as pariahs. Most of them secretly, too."

"Faust wore it at some point as a badge of honor. To him, the margins were inevitable if he was to work in any meaningful sense. For my part, I would've stayed had bureaucrats ceased their passive harassment."

"I became suspect of the idea of academic freedom. All the tools of the trade, all the conventions are there to help you. So it goes. But the professors are not as involved in their role of mentors as in their role of enforcers of the status quo. It's the same dreadful tribalism that you find elsewhere. Anyway, my rebellion intoxicated me, and only later was I able to go beyond mere vitriol."

"I want to remain a bit in your beginnings. Faustino seems to have been a typical nonconformist. How would you describe yourself, Dayana?"

"I fit loosely in the bitter type. While Faust here swelled his chest and made the ivory tower aware of his newfound freedom, I let my blood boil daily with the injustices of our country—and if I was up to it, the world. I hated seeing all the political commentators who warmed their chairs call for unity, civility, and concessions, as if the lower classes had their time and their means. I hated seeing a fractured left that had to resolve theoretical minutiae before reaching out its hand. More than anything else, I was insulted by the snail's pace of reform."

"Would both of you say the more intense feelings have been outgrown?"

"Maybe *refined* is a better word."

"I agree, I agree. It's not as if we were now reasonable, complying citizens who know better than to disrupt platitudes. Our initial impulse is still there. Years have only worked to understand when to vary the speed."

"Vary the speed? It's interesting that you say this, Dayana, because students have the impression that you're one of the last uncompromising intellectuals standing."

"I'm an activist, not an intellectual. This isn't pedantry. The word *intellectual* is inevitably tied to detachment, distance, impartiality—the very qualities I act against. By varying the speed I mean acquiring a sense of spiritual tempo. There are moments when certain efforts will land your foot in jail and moments when they'll land your foot in the door. I am uncompromising insofar as a major setback won't leave me in despair. But, again, you have to learn to read the atmosphere."

"Wouldn't you say detachment, distance, and impartiality help with this reading? A strong involvement with a cause can lead you astray, no? At least that seems to be one lesson of history."

"Those qualities lead to the pulpit. And rarely are you in a worse position than there. When you suddenly find yourself in a platform, the situation is clear—you've been made safe. People get the message. *It's okay to listen now; if she's here, she must've been approved in some way*. They'll cease to receive your words with all their edge and they'll have more reasons to readjust them."

"Do you agree with this, Faustino?"

"What Day describes is true, but maybe there's an opportune time to do it, as she might concede. Rarely will you reach through marginal outlets the number of people you'd reach through a consolidated platform. Then again, I understand it may be a detrimental way of doing it. This issue touches on that great problem of compromise."

"I think you avoided part of my question, Dayana. The intellectual qualities we spoke of can help avoid the pitfalls of dogmatism, wouldn't you say? I mean, they don't have to necessarily disorient you or make you a sell-out."

"They can. But I get the impression you may be thinking about their cultivation. And that's where I draw the line."

"Ha! Krumrie?"

"He's an instance, sure. And we've seen how emphatic he can be. He talks as if a misstep might ruin these little card-castles he builds in the air. He's cautious to the point of barrenness. But he calls this *intellectual integrity*."

"So you'd say their use must be intuitive."

"Not that left to chance. You learn the basics of *being reasonable* in childhood. Life throws lessons again and again. Philosophy, in a moderate dose, clears the outline and you're good to go."

"Cultivation really has no place?"

"As long as it is a weakening of will, no. Let's not pretend intellectual subtleties are causally inert."

"They have their place. Just not in political change."

"They have their place in a more just society, rather. Look at that! You caught a disagreement."

"We have yet to talk about your work. But I want to delve into this. There's consensus inside academia that 'useless' knowledge deserves promotion. The justifications are diverse, but most of them can be summed up by saying that it yields an edifying pleasure."

"As I said. Perhaps under other circumstances. Why would you dedicate years of your life to a dissertation suitable for ten lone scholars? These are commonly difficult subjects. I admit one can be floored by the abstruseness. Yet that brio could be used to work toward social betterment."

"Are those ten lone scholars to be shunned, then?"

"Yes. They'll be shunned in a manner that will never compare to that of marginalized people."

"Day is being severe. We can't let die the playful part of our tempers. Our neighbors, even in their precarious state, allow time for wondrous speculation."

"And that's exemplary! They ask for no institutionalization of their free play. Come on, Faust."

"I'm not talking about academy. I'm talking about giving a life over to that free play. Perhaps we haven't done so, but it should continue. I find it a respectable current. Or rather an undercurrent. Not many people want that."

"It has remained and will remain an activity that's supported on the shoulders of workers. You can't really dedicate your life to intellectual subtleties without the sheltering walls of an institution. It might be confined to afterhours—that much I'll concede."

"Now on to your work. Neil's been waiting for it."

"It feels a bit abrupt, I know, but many students have also been paying attention to this aspect of your lives. Dayana, you've limited yourself to publishing pamphlets, and it was barely last year that a book compilation materialized. Is this a political, aesthetic, or economical choice?"

"Definitely not aesthetic. I don't consider myself an artist. Neither would I go for economical. As you might know, Faust and I haven't ever published through a major house or a university press. Decades ago we went the haphazard route. A pamphlet of mine would be a couple of stapled pages and a book of Faust's would be spiral-bound ones. In recent years, we've got in touch with independent presses and also managed to publish online. The costs have never been forbidding. A political choice, then. I've always seen my pamphlets as field reports. I normally describe what worked and what didn't. I've never been interested in establishing a framework to move forward or in making predictions. Every political matter has the bad habit of filtering through the cracks of theory."

"In the prologue to your compilation you list a series of actions that have consistently worked throughout the years. Isn't that a framework?"

"Would you call your parents' life advice a framework? Someone could pin down the conceptual presuppositions and whatnot. I, however, am not interested in offering a theoretical outlook. It's a simple *this has worked, you should try it.*"

"What about the memoirs? Is there a framework there? Or anything like it?"

"That has been a strange undertaking. At first, I just wanted to wax lyrical, to indulge a little. Many stretches of my life have been meaningful in a way difficult to convey other than through the poetic. But I eventually couldn't continue. Exposing my life in its utterly private aspect simply wouldn't do. Why throw glitter now to the stand against injustice?"

"That's harsh. I'd call the rage in your pamphlets lyrical."

"Maybe. But I wouldn't call that poetic."

"There's a pamphlet Emily and I admire very much: *Unheard*. It's been seen as an eloquent apology of certain forms of violence. You call for decentralized, symbolic acts of destruction as a means to obtain an equal political footing with authority and also as a means to disrupt the complacent bickering of the average citizen. Though counterintuitive in its time, it has increased in relevance. Yet it's been used as an example by many professors and 'mainstream figures' of how to set back actual change. It may obtain a concession, but only in the short-term, at the cost of sullying the cause. Is this a reasonable concern?"

"It *is* a reasonable concern. Comfy mandarins specialize in reasonable concerns. I would say those concerns are the real setbacks. Imagine where workers would be had they waited for authority to lend them an ear and act on what was heard. Imagine where minorities would be had they waited for a place at the table. Disruption in its iconoclastic forms was, is, and will be the equalizer."

"Faustino, you, on the other hand, have mainly abandoned yourself to writing. It seems that Dayana and you converge on the vindication of experience. *The Imaginative Leap* does rely on something of a framework. You intend to plunge into literature setting aside its mystic garbs."

"Yes, yes. I belong to that curious tradition that extends from Protagoras to William James. It has yet to flourish."

"Why? Is this not proof of its maladjustment?"

"No. We have been slow to realize that the world surrounding us is rich enough not to require an aseptic duplicate. But once awakened, there is no going back to sterile illusions."

"Plato's tradition is sterile?"

"Taken as a succession of refinements of that other world, it isn't. Taken as a refinement of ours, it is."

"Where are we to leave the free play you championed, then?"

"Where it is. We can't have a blank slate. As one tradition gains momentum, the other will wane. It can't be expected to disappear: a passive flight from this world will endure so long as there are insistent difficulties."

"You called it respectable. And here you seem to call it spineless."

"All endeavors that seek to soothe our pains have a trace of probity, sterile as they may be. Let me contrast the traditions. Great as Plato's *topos hyperuranios* appears throughout the ages, it is wilfully exclusionist.

Its consoling heights are there for the few. It is fundamentally at odds with a sense of communion. And the few have delighted in further elevations and intricacies. Religion served as counterbalance. Yet its consolations have been dimming. Opposite, Protagoras faced not the awe-inspiring constellations, but the marble tides of Athens. He lent his hand to the common citizen and transmitted a feeling of camaraderie. His world is our world, and it boasts no heights."

"Why do you end with William James? Are there not many others who have continued?"

"None seem to strike the chord that he does. He was relentless against the heirs of Plato. He was relentless in what you called 'the vindication of experience.' He advanced for the remainder of his life an insight: if our concepts were insufficient before the world, it was only because of their overworked delicacy. They had been refined to suit the ethereal, not the jagged. They had been coddled in the static, not the fluid. Exhilarating. Yet James' successors were considerably more measured, more sophisticated. High-minded, if you will. That is why I believe the tradition has not flourished."

"Is it common for the next generation to yield?"

"It's rarely that simple. James himself owed much to Stuart Mill and Bain. There are epochs in which it is all on the brink of overflowing. The nineteenth century was exemplary in this respect."

"There is a pattern. But I figure historical recurrence is not your cup of tea."

"I'm flattered."

"Now, why confront literature? Is it not a breath of fresh air to see in it unbridled superstition?"

"As you know, there is a constant interplay between philosophy and literature. Novelists, dramatists, poets, and the like have focused intensely on the heavenly architecture. And owing to literature's somewhat freer tendencies, there you see an open scorn for earthbound communion, a more entrenched need for divinely ordained hierarchies."

"I would argue that our greatest poets were imbued with aristocratic beliefs. Dante defended divine rights, Shakespeare stood in awe of nobility, Goethe extolled innate gifts."

"I'm familiar with the procession. But it would be self-defeating to imagine that all greatness is past. Dante, Shakespeare, and Goethe dazzle me, but when I recover there is a lingering coldness. Cervantes, Johnson, and Chekhov, by planting their feet on the soil, communicate directly and deepen my sympathy."

"I sense a powerful moralistic vein."

"No, no. Beauty here resembles those moments in life in which you feel that at last you have reached another person, that at last there is an understanding other than the vague one attained from introspection."

"Has it been a life worth living? Has it not felt as if substantive change eluded both, as it has eluded many others?"

"I don't ask myself those questions. It's not for me to say."

"'Cast forth thy Act, thy Word, into the ever-living, ever-working Universe: it is a seed-grain that cannot die.'"

III

Drunk, upbeat, uninhibited, Emily and I approached Krumrie, who sat in a corner of the bar. He was alone. On the table, next to his collection of beers, the magazine shone.

"Why are you all mopey over here?"

Krumrie let out a faint laugh.

"It's fine. I'm fine. The . . . noise, yes, the noise is too much."

"How else would you celebrate, huh? Please tell me."

"I would not invite the whole, the faculty to a cramped bar."

"The whole faculty? Bah! Barely twenty persons, really."

Emily was in no hurry to ask about the interview. I couldn't wait.

"Did you read it?"

"Sure. There's some work in there. Interesting work. Points for Glenn's essay on Ramsey. I would've sworn he didn't pay it attention."

"What about your friends?"

"Same old. Day openly proudful, Faust openly reckless."

"Day is so sincere. I might've developed a crush. Faustino's all right."

"They also seem to be liked by their neighbors. Even more impressive."

"So much for independence."

"Ugh. I just don't get it. What's your problem?"

Krumrie let out another faint laugh.

"It's fine. I'm fine. I'm leaving now. It's late."

He stood, headed over to the counter, and returned for his coat.

"The magazine, Krumrie."

"They both asked about you. They even shared a couple of memories you wouldn't. *Affectionate* memories. I thought you should know."

"They care. Just the other day they said to me, 'We'd respect you, cherish your company, even if you'd let time pass you by.'"

He imitated their mannerisms and left. I was about to discuss the tone, but Emily stared absently at the table. The remnants of a beer had spilled over the magazine.

All the Works That My Hands Had Wrought

I

I AM AN UNREMARKABLE MAN. The limit of my physical and intellectual endowment is quite clear. My attention span is rather lacking; it is equipped to deal with breezy conversations and fifteen-minute readings. Sure, I can go beyond that, but not without an immense effort. My memory is poor; it is fond of mixing things up. I am a slow learner. I have no natural affinity for abstraction. My motor coordination has brought me many problems. I am short, scrawny, and slightly bald. In spite of these deficiencies, I lived my life as if I were a Renaissance man.

Throughout my childhood, I received plenty of compliments. They were, however, the nice-sounding, empty compliments any moderately well-behaved boy heard daily. My teachers reveled in the pronunciation of dignified words such as *gifted* and *talented*. It was not only a matter of euphonic exultation: the rate at which they threw these terms spoke about their own competence as educators. Not a soul cared whether it was plausible to have fifteen exceptional students in a class of seventeen.

My parents' praise was the one I craved most. It did not come from the assembly line of school panegyrics. Hope infused every parental word with sincerity.

I understood soon enough that knowledge in itself was useless and uninteresting. It could not compare to the sparkle of exhibition.

With regard to athletic activities, I faced an insurmountable obstacle; even so, I would get here and there a word of approval. Things were fine as long as one made no overt display of incompetence.

Was I conscious of my mediocrity? Yes. I owed this to Ethan. While he received the cookie-cutter flattery we all did, he did not respond to it in the same way. I am not one to mystify others, but Ethan had a disinterestedness that distanced him from the rest. We never spoke to each other. Perhaps talking with him would have made it clear that he was as dull as everyone else. Yet I am incapable of seriously considering this possibility. I was not an Ethan. But it is important to insist that no one appeared to notice.

If nothing crashes violently against our fanciful beliefs, they will root themselves until they acquire the status of truths. I was cautious not to talk about Ethan with anyone.

II

It was no hard work keeping alive the flame of adulation as I entered adolescence. But I began to feel inadequate when those around me quickly ignored my achievements. At least those who had a voice— teachers were nonentities. To stand out genuinely, I had to show off either in sports or in flirting. I could not waste time, so I undertook to squeeze out of my cast-iron lack of charisma.

I stumbled through all possible realms of flirtation available to a fifteen-year-old. In the process, I managed to collect myriad hugs and some kisses. I saw this as progress, and more than one of my classmates agreed. The problem: I was nowhere near the top. For instance, Dave bragged day in and day out that he had already seen and touched the breasts of five girls, and Jake could not let an opportunity go to boast how he had almost lost his virginity thrice.

Whenever I felt I was catching up, someone would bring out a new exploit. I had seen it as a competition since the beginning, but I could not have imagined how things would turn out when the rest did. Badinage turned into merciless ridicule. One conversation stands out. We were all at Jake's house hours before a party. I was seventeen years old.

"You should have seen her face. I mean, really. I've perfected the technique. Fucking Satriani would have been proud. I swear I was sweep-picking down there."

Everyone was roaring with laughter. Jake knew how to entertain; he was the heart of the group. But as soon as he put his eyes on me, I knew what was coming.

"Say, Andrew, how's your technique?"

"Pretty great, to be honest."

Confidence did not become me. My voice paled next to his.

"Then you've made a girl orgasm, right?"

"Sure."

"Tell us all about it."

"Well, remember Angie? A week ago we were in her room. We started kissing, so I slowly took off her blouse. She has some fine knockers."

It was ridiculous. I had no flare. Jake went ahead with gusto.

"You took off her *blouse*? Damn. Are you sure she didn't orgasm right then? I'm kidding, man. Tell me, how big were these *knockers* you speak of?"

Dave was cracking up. He joined in.

"Come on, Andy. You sound so fucking awkward. I'm sure you've seen a girl naked. But I'm having trouble believing you've done much else. Hey, look, you can tell us. Being a virgin is kind of cool, you know. You're helping this group be inclusive. Fantastic, if you ask me."

I let them go on. I *was* a virgin. By acting defensive, I would have made it a known fact. It was better for me to laugh it off.

As I staggered, Jake bustled. I endured this dynamic for years. When I finally lost my virginity (twenty-one), he had been fucking as if he had had a vision of imminent impotence. My self-worth was lost.

I never stopped thinking about distinction through academic performance. That had been, after all, my gateway to praise. And it meant much more to my peers in college than it did to those in high school. But distinction was now difficult to attain. I did not want to return to the old days of rote memorization. So I waited (sadly competing with Jake and friends) for anything that could simplify things. Then I met Colin.

III

Colin Grove was an adjunct professor of English at my university and a notorious character. There was no candidate for tenure as definite as he. A seemingly affable guy, he talked with students after class most of the time. I knew he would be my ticket out of anonymity and dejection.

I first talked to Colin at a reunion of sorts in his apartment. A mutual friend had invited me to go with him. To my amazement, there were six persons there. I felt embarrassed when they paused their conversation and greeted us. They were all sitting on a relatively well-kept sectional sofa. Colin was in the middle. On the left, there was a couple whom I had seen many times at the university; they were usually chasing professors. On the right, cramped, there were three guys in their late twenties, about Colin's age. The coffee table in the center was packed with beer cans and ashtrays, all of them supported by books of varying condition. At the top of the pile, covered with ashes that had not found their way, an honors thesis was noticeable.

We took two chairs from a table nearby.

"Why don't you go grab a beer? We have some in the fridge."

Colin stared at us as if his comment were not a cordial gesture but an order. We went over to the kitchen, which was just a few steps away. The fridge had only beers and a jar of mayonnaise. This first impression did not match my expectations. We grabbed the beers and sat.

The conversation resumed. It had to do with David Foster Wallace's reception of Roth, Mailer, and Updike. In a matter of minutes, I understood all the fanfare that surrounded Colin. His intervention seamlessly progressed to a full-blown monologue. The sheer quantity of names and concepts that were intertwined baffled me. But I found more impressive that no one was irritated. Quite the contrary, everyone looked pleased.

Out of nowhere, Colin broke the monologue and addressed me. He wanted my opinion on the matter. This forced interlude did not strike me as charitable. He sought to bolster his words by way of contrast. I threw in one or two names that he had not mentioned. Almost machine-like, he dismissed their pertinence.

Before the evening ended, when everyone was scattered chatting in groups, Colin went out of his way to invite me to take one of his courses. He was not the same person who had written me off earlier. He was attentive. This was my first acquaintance with his showmanship, a quality I came to covet and admire.

IV

I took Colin's course on early twentieth-century fiction. As a professor, he was conspicuously didactic and tolerant with students. If someone made the classic let-me-repeat-most-of-what-you-said-with-only-three-or-four-new-adverbs/adjectives-added comment, he smiled and found a way to enrich the blatant attempt at appearing engaged. In his face were no traces of scorn. At most, I saw him a bit exasperated by the occasional I-read-last-night-in-a-hurry-an-interesting-article/essay-that-changed-my-worldview student, who tested the soundness of his discovery with a snide interruption.

I spent most afternoons at Colin's apartment. He made it a routine to invite me over. I had gained his trust by being a spectator of his invectives against all. They had reached an alarming virulence. Those around him were, without exception, dim-witted ultracrepidarians.

To speak about a stark contrast between the professor and the man would be naïve. He relished the power he had over students. He knew that not a single person in the room had the ability to contradict him plausibly. He was at the summit, peering with a mollified dignity into the daft world of those below him. With his colleagues, such a position was untenable. He had to convince them of his eminence in private. And he had to be cautious. An encyclopedic understanding of the feuds and affinities within the department was paramount for him to bash leisurely.

All the Works That My Hands Had Wrought

If this paltriness were all there was to Colin Grove, I would have stopped frequenting him in a matter of days. But for some reason (probably related to his ego) he was willing to share the basics of his showmanship. He reserved each day half an hour to discuss my advances.

I had wished merely to stand out. Colin made sure that I went much further. I was awakened from a dogmatic slumber in which my discipline established the limits of what I could use. I acquired, unobstructed by forced modesty, a clear view of knowledge at large. In a burst of energy, I became interested in art, history, linguistics, philosophy, psychology, neuroscience, biology, chemistry, physics, mathematics, music, film, chess, politics, economics, pop culture, etc. It was outrageous. I gave no thought to my aptitudes. I spilled nearly all the contents while trying to imbibe them frenetically, for I had never felt such thirst and imagined it was fleeting.

Colin tested me in class. I was still far from him, yet I was able to conjure up a semblance of his flashiness. At least enough to start making a reputation. As my confidence increased, I made my presence felt wherever I was. There was hesitance at the beginning—a perceptive professor could call out my gauzy expostulations and ruin it all. But this did not happen. Instead, I was commended for my audacity. Colin was delighted. His "experiment" (an epithet he used half-jokingly) had been a success.

After that busy academic year, there was a certain camaraderie between Colin and me. We regularly went for drinks with his actual friends. And the pedant who had once used me as a prop now took his time weighing my opinions. I convinced myself that there were no reasons for him to be acting. I even arrived at the belief that I was exceptional and thus more than worthy of being considered his equal. When it came to self-appraisal, I was inordinately fond of these miraculous leaps.

V

Colin offered me a teaching position in a community college right at the time I was about to finish my undergraduate program. He had a connection there. My reluctance came from a moment of clarity. I was unwilling to expose myself, to risk being found out. I had, as with everything else, a fuzzy knowledge of the subject I was expected to teach. But Colin was adamant. So Fundamentals of Writing it would be.

Fortunately for my fragile self-esteem, students were lazy and lifeless, as were my colleagues. How I thrived in this swamp of vapidness! Unobstructed, unchallenged, and coddled by mediocrity.

Gliding smoothly through academic life, I rummaged the preceding years. My ascent had been considerable, and everyone in my immediacy was conscious of it. I felt a sting when thinking about those I had left behind; they could not see this. And I thought about one particular person—Jake. I had not been able to outdo him in his terrain, but in mine I certainly had a stupendous advantage. This conviction led me to entertain a ridiculous idea.

Jake and I had been out of touch with each other for three years. The last thing I knew about him was that he had undertaken a business degree. I did not expect him to accept my invitation for a meeting. A week later I was waiting for him at a bar near the university.

I was nervous. I did my best to hide it, but any time I saw a guy with a confident gait I found myself awkwardly trying to sit in an aloof way. He was fifteen minutes late and grinned as soon as he saw me. I extended my hand. He grabbed my shoulders and stared at me as if he were about to break bad news.

"Andrew, pal. I see you're still not a fan of the gym, right?"

I did not smile or laugh. By doing this, I would have given him the upper hand. He did not laugh, either. He sat down and ordered a drink.

"What did you say you were studying? Books or what?"

Every word of his had a sardonic tone. I wondered why he kept this attitude up when there were no people around to amuse. Was he amusing himself?

I was stiff during the conversation. I had planned to humble him with countless asides and ironic remarks, but his insouciance disarmed me. My eyes glowed at the prospect of lobbing an indirect jab to his ego—Petrarch or Pascal? And then I saw a prophylactic smirk, a ponderous elevation of his chin, a sinuous eyebrow at the brink of raising, fingers ready to tap a jazzy tune on the wooden table. He reeked of complacency.

It was only after several drinks that I had the nerve to start flaunting my triumphs, no longer capable of subtlety. I paid no attention to his body language. I just went on and flooded him with poorly chosen words.

After saying it all, I finished my drink and, without much reason, laughed. He sat there, quiet, looking at his full glass. He shook it and smiled at the sound of the ice scraping against the translucent walls. It was unusual seeing him concentrating on a purposeless activity. I knew he was as drunk as I was. He kept shaking the glass and then decided to down his drink. He did this calmly, enjoying every drop. There was a sensuality to it that made me feel uncomfortable. When he finished, he put the glass back on the table and pointed to his watch.

"Andrew, Andy, Andrés, Andrea. I must leave you."

He was not slurring.

"What? Let's have another one."

"Oh, no, no. I think we've had enough of each other."

He leaned forward in a vaguely menacing way. His lids twitched while he tried to stare me down. I said nothing.

"Wouldn't you agree?"

He slapped my shoulder and left his hand there.

"I don't mean to offend you, Andrea. But there's always been something about your voice that irks me. And by god, I've heard it this afternoon nonstop. It makes me happy that you have found a niche where others can pretend to take you seriously. Oh, hold on. What if they're like *you*? Yeah, yeah, that makes more sense. Curious little men who stare at their books as if there were nothing else—until an ass walks by, that is. Then they look askance and memorize it, so they can later jack off to it in the privacy of their comfy libraries."

He let go of my shoulder, got up, and threw some dollars on the table.

"I was curious to see you, Andy. Curiosity isn't bad, right? You're the same thing. Anyway, I threw in extra cash. Go ahead and drink something strong for me, will you? Who knows? If you keep it up, maybe you'll get rid of that voice. Then we could have another talk later on."

I sat in silence and watched him leave. I left the bar an hour later, tottering away with the light of consciousness about to leave a dead weight under the rain.

VI

Days after the incident, I felt proud of witnessing the loss of Jake's aplomb. He had spoken about a subject that exceeded him. And he had been drunk. Moreover, he had focused on a shallow aspect of my life. He had measured it with that all-important deity of his. So I carried on.

My reputation at the community college reached new peaks. Colleagues and students had no use now for the distance of respect and offered themselves to the subdued pleasures of sycophancy. I was offered the opportunity to write a textbook on grammar. I obliged and gave the news to Colin.

His reaction was hostile, hyperbolic, and damningly personal. He said I was a vessel of incompetence, not even a dilettante on the matter; he went off on a tangent regarding the fierce efficacy of disgusting traits' reproduction; he advised me to have probity and decline the offer. This was one reproach too many. I held nothing back in my answer.

I cannot say our relationship soured—he was quick to clarify that day we had none; I was one in a long row who pined for his attention and mentorship.

He had been embittered by the Kafkaesque delay of his tenure. His opportunities shrank while mine rose. The quality of these differences did not matter to him. It was the mere image of his stagnation and my movement that called forth his animosity.

VII

My life was finally free from the influence of two towering figures. It was a matter of time for the provinciality of my recognition to reach cosmopolitan heights. Intoxicated by the ineluctable payment of what was owed me, I marched through the crippling narrowness of daily life with optimism. All minor accomplishments were blown out of proportion; they signaled what was to come.

As each year piled over the other, doings did not—they scattered. I had been going in circles, too immersed in the contemplation of my endurance. At last, I was burned out. I embraced stasis. I kept my ego well fed with carefully tailored memories.

Again and again, I visited my university days. They had an unnatural vastness that lured me. The rest of my life was a postscript.

I decided one day to open the textbook on grammar, the only book I had ended up publishing, which had long ago gone out of print. Reading the first pages, I came to terms with my mediocrity. I had no energy left to excuse myself. It was laden with glaring mistakes, confident in its wrongheaded tone, interspersed with droll observations—an all-around tribute to charlatans everywhere.

I finished it in one sitting.

I remembered Ethan. I made myself a cup of coffee and looked for a marker.

Remnant

YAKOV has a peculiar way of worrying, eyes always set on immortality. He walks as if hunched by the weight of yet-to-be-born thousands, who all have a claim to some part of his being. He speaks as if hesitance were to ruin a potential aphorism, believing his colleagues variants of Boswell. And, of course, he is cautious not to bring too much attention upon himself; long ago he must have resolved that to play the dandy would be unbecoming of someone as plain-featured as he. But has it been wise to play the misanthrope, to sigh at the view of a living world?

I caught a glimpse of his green checkered shirt at one of Karla's gatherings. Most of the attendees had an academic connection to philosophy, so it is easy to imagine the atmosphere: no gravitas, only irreverence. It was an act of unusual boldness to maintain a scowl amid the grins. And there he was, atypical, gripping his cup of anything but wine, exchanging the occasional word with Karla, who took her time before presenting us.

"So you do care once in a while, sæti. Look, here's your match."

"It's nothing personal. I like to work at night. What can one do?"

"This is a habit of his, Yakovlevich. Silva is rude that way."

"Pay no attention. You must know her by now."

"Silva. Like the poet?"

"You like literature?"

"Ha! That is an understatement."

"I do, yes."

"Refreshing. One hears about it only in journals. Mainly as a way to illustrate some obscure philosophical point."

"Is that right? I guess you enjoy it, then."

"There's a caveat: when I have the time."

"Oh, Silva, always the gentleman. It's nice to see both of you share some common ground. I will be leaving. I'm positive I've heard whatever is to follow."

I expected Karla's quirky jab to lighten the mood, but Yakov did not budge. His seriousness, however, contrasted with his voice, which grew high-pitched as we delved deeper into other subjects.

"I would rather live like your namesake, yes."

"Now I see what captured Karla's imagination."

"What do you mean?"

"She gets bored of the chatter. Have you had a chance to speak with someone other than her?"

"No."

"Great. You would be bombarded with Socratic irony. 'Ah, *intensity*, that is a rather opaque term. Do we not *also* use it to describe *trifles*? Please do *tell* how is it that its use in poetry differs.' And so on. They don't really care. At least not in my experience. What matters is showing that you're as confused as any bumbling idiot."

"I am familiar with the type. I studied philosophy years ago."

"That seems to me an important detail. Why didn't you mention it?"

"I gave it up after a while. It is a trivial part of my life. Nothing good came of it."

"And here you are, speaking with a specialist in Dewey's philosophy of mind."

Yakov's faux-deep voice crept back and not much else was said.

Even if our conversation was too casual then, there were details that in hindsight appear significant: the deliberate pause between each sentence, the subtle nudge toward time-honored obsessions, the fluctuations of tone, the adamantine scowl. I liked him despite the I-would-rathers.

We saw each other only at Karla's gatherings, which meant that any possibility of friendship was low. He always sat in the same corner, near the same chair. And Karla was always hovering by. She talked with him for long intervals, offered him drinks and underlined books. I had imagined he was laconic with her, but no. Were her displays of affection maternal, fraternal, or romantic? Hard to say. As soon as I went for maternal, she played with his hair; for romantic, she annoyed him with some practical joke; for fraternal, she rubbed his shoulder while gazing at him with condescending eyes. In all instances, he seemed uncomfortable. Suddenly, I had before me another telling detail, or rather an explanation. His seriousness was not organic. It was a way of dealing with his body. I believed my conjectures to be sound.

"But these intellectual types are always a bit awkward, right? Look around."

"They are no more awkward than anyone at any party. Aside from the extroversion machines that make a point of their presence, of course."

"You mean that? Both of us are living proof of those *not very comfortable in their skin*."

"I disagree."

"If there are extroversion machines, surely there are introversion machines."

"Yes, and there are none here."

"Okay, I'll be blunter. Laughing is a sign of being socially at ease. How often do you laugh?"

"I understand. Your example was not inadvertent."

"This is not personal. Really, it isn't."

"If you have to know, I find humor in simple things. People falling, for example. Otherwise, it feels contrived."

I could not take these words at face value; he was patently irritated. But they left me more curious. Here was an educated man defending his dignity by appealing to slapstick.

Karla thought little of my speculations. She gave him greater leeway than I did. The roulette kept spinning—maternal, fraternal, romantic.

"I've known him for years. You've just known him for months. So I have the upper hand."

"How unphilosophical, K. You're actually at a disadvantage. You're too close. You are more familiar with the way he wants to portray himself. I have a clearer view."

"Silly, silly Silva. What do you know about him? Go ahead, tell me."

"Let's see. He says he loves literature, poetry specifically. I think that has more to do with trying to distance himself from *professors of philosophy*. He says he also loves philosophy, analytical specifically. Easy: he doesn't want to be classed with soft-minded *littérateurs*. He says he cares little for worldly success. Easier: he wants to distance himself from *us*."

"Very articulate handling of stereotypes. But I'm sorry to say that Yakovlevich is absent."

"Is he? Illuminate me, then."

"You see, something important is missing. He's a person, not an abstraction. But you can't find this obviously true. The fact that you don't know a thing about his life messes with your attempts at explanation. And this applies to all you've said about his seriousness too."

"That's why you're struggling for tenure."

"Oh, Silva, what would I do without your idiotic jokes?"

"Believe I'm not unlike the Yakovs of the world."

"You're a person, Silva, no doubt about that."

Karla did emphasize a partial truth. I knew almost nothing of Yakov's life. This was a subject toward which his nudges never pointed. He had studied philosophy once and wrote poetry (and perhaps some philosophy). Yet life isn't just a series of exercises for memory; it also comprises our day-to-day thoughts and foibles. Our conversations were part of his life, make-believe and everything. Though slight, I had a hold of Yakov.

Predictably, Karla got tired of the crowded evenings. She moved out to a smaller place and rescaled the old routine. Twice a month Yakov, Irene, Thomas, and I went over. Irene and Thomas were an obvious choice. Thomas was a close friend of Karla's in high school. He became an entrepreneur (therapy on demand, test preparation, café, used bookstore). Irene, whom he married, studied law and helped out early on. Their cosmopolitan sensibilities worked perfectly to check everybody's provincial attitudes but Yakov's. And in this more intimate atmosphere I grasped what was missing.

"Where's the lure of posterity? I suspect it always follows a pattern of disappointment. In an arid life it must be a comforting mirage."

"A mirage? Just look at us, continuing the genuflection to heroes."

"Right. But they will never taste this posthumous glory. The present you *can* taste."

"I take it, Thomas, that you're making a case for your life."

"No. I'm not in the business of justifying my zest."

"Any thoughts, Yakovlevich?"

"I disagree. The scope of the present is poor. One can reach out to few. Casting your work into the future guarantees sympathetic ears, however disagreeable."

"Does that matter other than in an abstract way? It is a tortuous route toward pleasure."

"It is vaguely related to pleasure. I would rather believe it has to do with multiplying one's possibilities. Here, I can be a modest number of Yakovs: Silva's, Karla's, Thomas's, Irene's. There, I will be boundless."

"Which is pleasurable."

"No. It is a metaphysical thirst. I resist tying it to something as homely as pleasure."

"You see, this is the type of discourse I find baffling. It's relentlessly abstract. Life is left aside."

"Life. That word's connotations are baffling—sense stimulation, excess, haste."

"Energy. That is it."

Those were the usual disagreements between Thomas and Yakov. And so long as I didn't intervene, Yakov remained polite. He knew I pursued questions of theory until they collapsed into psychology. His psychology. This subject, posterity, proved important. There was the center I sought. So I led Thomas and waited for their discussions. Thomas shared the way in which I approached reality. Both of us lived oblivious to a future judgment. We had no invisible beads hanging from our necks.

Yakov's religious upbringing became steadily visible. His father insisted on God's watchfulness. Soon Yakov felt the inhibition of his will. All acts and thoughts had an audience. What's more: a discriminating and uptight audience. If he swore, his impious words were heard through the chambers of heaven. If he bore ill-will, the heat of his heart enraged the overseer. The prison formed in childhood is a perennial prison.

The novelty of Yakov ceased, and Thomas had no interest left for more facts of life. Irene, owing to her politeness, was the only one who asked about this or that biographical detail.

The gatherings also came to an abrupt end when Yakov was hired as a teacher of poetry in some nameless high school thirty minutes east of Palm Springs. Now he was in the habit of inviting us to visit separately. It was in one of these visits that I felt compelled to inquire at length about his ways.

We met at a charming little park, unlike most you find in California. There were no traces of Park Advisory Council regulations, just an entanglement of wooden benches, rustic seesaws, and bull thistle. There, Yakov sat on a trunk, a navy blue rundown briefcase at his side. He was drinking from a thermos.

"How long have we known each other?"

"Three, four years? I don't count."

"Strange. This has been something of an impersonal friendship."

"Always from your end."

"I . . ."

"Disagree? I'd imagine."

"Your eyes are too open. I feel myself a case study in your presence."

"You seem to wish for that treatment. I'm sure you're self-aware."

"We all are when we understand that others also devote their time to remembrance."

"In a bookish sense, Yakov."

"I forget. You and Thomas, ever the lovers of clear-cut distinctions."

"You've been in touch with him?"

"No. I wish him well, though."

"Anyway, bookish, deliberate. I never bought your idea of possibilities."

"I was not selling, clearly."

"You are unambiguous."

"That would be foolish of me, wouldn't it? I'm not that coarse. But I've been meaning to make a concession to you."

"I'm here."

"I do have a pronounced sense of discomfort. It has followed me around most of my life. That is all I can concede. I don't understand its nature. Your conjectures are as good as any."

"There's a lot to work with."

"Unfortunately, I am skeptical about the uses of autobiography. Right here, talking with you, I have a guess. I am too in love with the past in which I had no business existing. The past of the poets, of the novelists, of the philosophers. Yes. I am not concerned with the undeveloped present, with the would-be monuments. Yes. But let us stop. This is all there is to it. An old-school egoist."

With a mystifying nod he settled the matter. We had a pleasant afternoon, perhaps the very first one that I enjoyed in his company. And more would follow.

So, Yakov, are you wise? Only if the real lies elsewhere.

Roulette

From Eveline I learned exuberance of spirit and indifference to the self-congratulating affectation of morals.

From the irrepressible dissatisfaction of Samuel, rejection of all middling concessions and a headstrong patience.

From Eliza, pliancy and an ear for the rhythms that match the vital beat bestowed upon me by nature; and further, leisurely travel between the extremes of abundance and scarcity.

From Eliezer, care for my fellows, and to know that a retreat toward supposedly higher spheres means desertion of fertile grounds.

From Uriel, endurance, not as mere gymnastics, but as harmony with an inner wholeness, and to want more according to its secret laws, aware, always aware, that the pangs of unfulfillment have no room here.

From Silas, not to shun the small, for the most sublime rests on it and acquires its dignity piece by piece; and to have tried my hand in painting, so as to see how even the small rests on elaborate patterns that make of it another sublime.

From Leah I received the impression that the plurality of worlds offered by books must be enjoyed without hope of wisdom, for their laws obey the idiosyncratic regularities of their makers; and from her I learned haste is the proper road of intuition.

From Alexander, to furnish my purpose with all manner of adornments, so as to find relief in the midst of barren tracts; and to be always different, in pursuit of the many-hued shades bestrewn by nature; and from him I learned that friendship is eminently the understanding of frailty.

From Cassandra, a freewheeling disposition, and the example of a family governed in a sympathetic manner, and the idea of living without the turn of a sculpture; and to tolerate the outnumbering partialities of others: she readily adapted her convictions in order to witness the flowering of a foreign and truly personal vision, thus carrying a richer scope than most.

From Matthew the autodidact, to refrain from pedantry, that poison of unoriginal minds, and to venture forward, cautious only of having firm ground under my feet, which means not approval of authority but rather assimilation; and to find wonder in the arrangement of a thoroughly intimate canon.

From Ivan I learned to observe the numerous ways in which all throughout the social hierarchy everyone simulates what is expected and waits for no one to bother, however miserable the masquerade.

From Stella the pessimist, to seek moments of isolation and temper the flow of chatter, for the spiritual expenditure is never quite compensated.

From Mauricio, to give up the mirage of infallibility, dear drug of self-appointed sages and prophets; and to be thankful to those who choose to see us unvarnished by neighboring fictions; and to remember the crack of which Emerson speaks.

From esteemed Edmund, to leave behind the regal robes that compel me to advance immaculate decrees, which have the mean advantage of dealing with imaginary setups; and through him I learned that trial and error maintains mind and will active, almost united; I learned from him also that any suggestion of regularity must not be taken for a clear-cut inducement to abstraction, and that much is elastic.

From Antonio I learned to trust an impossibly persistent though mellow optimism. I discerned that much of his life was spent in hardship, struggling to gain what others had since birth, and that people were fond of ridiculing the awkwardness he had earned through his plight. He suffered and yet could not contain his laughter, which resonated without the least intimation of bitterness. He had also the art of forgetting the trivial affronts that crowd even the imposing souls.

In my nearest colleague I observed a readiness to transform any place in which he worked into a community, and a love for his religion so deep that no other worldview could be meager enough not to awaken his interest and sympathy. And I observed that his energies flagged, as is natural, yet had no decisive impact on the overall arc of his trajectory, so that one asked whether it would culminate within a lifetime. I observed too his devotion to many outdated creeds, from which he somehow extracted honey long thought to lie elsewhere. There was in him a veritable Pelagian, amused if somewhat worn by the world's unremitting coarseness and happy acquiescence to self-mortification as atonement for calculated cruelty.

Sleep Decades

To a now untraceable patchwork of circumstances I am indebted for having a close-knit family that transcends blood, even if at times its members fade. Further, I am thankful that no palpable fences were put on my road, for it seems that those around me wisely judged the effort as fruitless. I thank too the resilience of a distant memory that soothes me at mysterious intervals: a student, of whom I have lost the name, approaches me, calm and forthright; he talks of many things; I retain only the vivid gestures and an aimless utterance: we are great in spite of ourselves.

Among apathetic young adults at the institute.

Boca de Iguanas

As **THE VIVID TONES** of ocean and sand gave way to a more downcast layer, the heat began to fade. Far-off, bronze spots clustered toward every conceivable entrance, carrying fluorescent lines. An unassuming breeze enveloped the coast and altered the rhythm of the waves. The once muffled sound of the tide surged in a form that overwhelmed the senses.

Attuned to the distinct pulses of my body, I maundered in and out of sleep. A giggle broke the trance. I opened my eyes to the sight of Liliana and Sandra struggling to light a bonfire. Reclining a few steps from me on a cooler, Adriana could not contain her amusement.

"Come on, girls! You have the alpha males out for beers."

Her legs and arms were swathed in streaks of black, which suggested she had already given a shot at helping.

"Hey, you're awake. Why not assist the ladies?"

I stood up and went over to see what could be done. Before I had chance to catch a glimpse, Liliana and Sandra yelled and danced with unbearable glee—a bright red tongue quivered in parallel. Not to feel too useless, I threw some sticks into the fire.

"There you go! Impossible without him. Right, girls?"

In the midst of delight, they had no ears for anything other than their chant. I went back and snickered.

"Always late. Not useful for drinks, not useful for fire."

Adriana grabbed a beer that was hidden below one of her thighs and passed it.

"I don't like drinking alone."

Its taste was tolerable. Liliana and Sandra stayed close to their triumph and made no attempt to lure us. They cuddled against a log and prattled. Adriana threw some grains of sand on my knees, more as part of an abrupt brooding than as a playful gesture; there had always been something patently physical in her reveries.

"We've barely talked."

The last word straggled, intimating disappointment. I turned my face in her direction; she was staring at her toes, which sank deeper into the sand.

"Don't you think?"

"You've spent most of the time with Isaac. I can't really talk to both of you."

She cupped her hands, filled them to the brim with sand, and covered what was left of my knees.

"Why is it a big deal?"

"Because it happened."

She observed Liliana and Sandra, who were now asleep. The purple tinge of the evening swallowed almost all their bodies. Their faces glowed.

"You're both important. I've always refused to toss things away just because. I still have all my shells."

"I'd like to agree, but . . . why be a hypocrite? I've been in his place."

Boca de Iguanas

I began to feel a slight cold. A strong wind blew and the waves sparkled. Distance clothed boats here and there as will-o'-the-wisps. I was bemused and looked once again at Adriana. Her big eyes betrayed a similar ignorance.

She rose and dropped her shawl. Her short olive legs shone despite the faint reach of the fire. They were robust, much livelier than I remembered. She walked until an outline replaced her. She stretched and, even with the ocean as backdrop, her movements were lithe; they bespoke a successive bloom. This was an aspect of her with which I was thoroughly unfamiliar.

I knew not whether to join or stay put. The decision, however, was taken for me. Isaac's boisterous screams saturated the air. He carried a box of beers. Close by, Philip lit a cigarette and waved.

Though I regretted the noise, I had to admit calm was meant as a transition; all the trip Isaac's and Philip's cheerful tempers were the norm. Liliana and Sandra woke up, encouraged the commotion, and put on some music. Adriana shed at once her pensive vein and brightened.

I grabbed another beer. I could not share in their elation. I simply looked, without acknowledgement. This oyster-like seclusion was a habit of mine when faced with temptation; far from virtue, to say the least, since it had its roots in an unrealistic though cunning desire: attention. I waited for Adriana to draw nearer, to enliven me and realize, as the night passed into dawn, that she had nothing figured out. But to no avail. She spoke eagerly with Isaac, caressed and taunted him, spilled beer over his shirt owing to her ebullience. I sought comfort in her rare glances, reduced to a meanness I had not felt up till then.

Philip sat beside me after a while. He seemed dazed.

"You see those palms over there? We caught a bunch of teenagers trying to bring the coconuts down. You wouldn't believe their determination: vagrants in a land of plenty, for all I know. Once they did, they couldn't crack them open. And as they were about to, some policeman in a silly scooter chased them away. Private property, I think."

"How long did you watch?"

"Lost track. It really was something. And I'll be honest: I myself thought of going over for some coconuts when we just got here. Scooter cops didn't cross my mind. Isaac wanted to lend the kids a hand, but it was easy to discourage him. His anarchy dissolves when he hits the stop button."

"Why didn't you say yes?"

"It's just a bunch of kids having fun. We would've added uncalled-for seriousness."

Not much later, Liliana was plastered, and a torpid Sandra guided her to their tent. Adriana and Isaac went for a dive. Philip, who now made every unnecessary effort to appear lucid, got a hold of his backpack and pulled out a bottle of wine.

"I brought you this present."

The slur of his voice doubled us up.

"Let's go over there. I wanna watch the waves. Hear them."

We took turns drinking. Philip pointed toward the couple.

"Havin' fun. You wouldn't guess they're this happy."

The wine was consummately cheap. And its intensity quickly knocked Philip out. The wind was at its strongest, yet the warmth I had achieved by then harbored me. There was no sight of the boats. Only the amorous silhouettes leapt through the shadows. I was tired.

I lay down. As I tried to grasp the meaning of Philip's last comment, a newfound distance between the sky and me materialized. The stars were dim and threatened to wither in the growing gulf. I fought the urge to wake Philip up. It was Adriana I had in mind. And thus I staggered around in the darkness of my conscience.

Love—

THE OLD BRANCHES still reach high. I am reminded of last year's thought: our conjoined misery will survive the tree's course through the calendar. Somehow an outward signpost slightly dissipated the vagueness of prolonged grief. Yet it also sharpened the loss. I longed for my wife's fingers drifting across my back as I watched the twigs vibrate, I longed for the contours of her waist freewheeling against my hands as I watched the trunk sway, I longed for the thread of hair caressing my lips as I watched the leaves droop. And then the sense of guilt, for the fragments that held me in such a trance belonged to a withering woman with whom I had shared the better part of my life.

Five years I had tended to an increasingly severe depression. It had no identifiable beginning. Or if it did, we were not aware of it. The liveliness of her manner dimmed in a strange progression. Her highs were always attaining the same height, but her lows found newer and newer depths. Until the highs became a tolerable apathy, then nothing. Of course there was a nagging and vain feeling that I was to blame, though she was quick to brush off my misgivings. Pills soon answered our concerns.

At no point had she surrendered to the inertia that clogs the affections. The very simple language we had developed unconsciously in brighter days broadened under the weight. I suppose there was a mixture of sincerity and effort. The psychiatrist once explained to her that an emotion is the effect of a bodily change, not the other way around. But I responded with a growing tepidness. She had long retreated from the more demanding intimacy: a kiss was faintly sustained, a caress led nowhere and met no reaction. The matter was settled when I pushed too hard.

"This is tiring. It is one more problem to think about."

"What? A problem?"

"Yes. I've really wanted it to be something else. But it is a problem now."

"Something else?"

"A passing thought, a moment of weakness, I don't know."

"We're talking about something that makes both of us happy."

"Yes, it did. But, I mean, look at me. I'm tired. I simply can't. I have no other way of saying it. And I guess I'm glad that we're finally talking about it. I can't. No. I just, no."

"Don't you feel a buildup when we're laughing, when we have a moment to breathe?"

"I'm still here, Ruben. And I enjoy those things. They are enough. They are what I need."

I felt an urge to talk about my own needs and whatnot, even if I was opening myself to accusations of selfishness. Yet I was struck by the way she then held my hand. There was no strength, no warmth. One could scarcely imagine it was the extremity of anything living. Indeed, the accusations would have been grounded. I was possessed by a guilt that would come to be inexorably linked to my lust.

Duty compelled me forward insofar as it remained concrete. I found a measure of nourishment in our surface contacts. A kiss, a hug, a laugh. But that too decayed, leaving us with words. My obligation became abstract. And I hesitated again and again, relentlessly thrown backward. Since the present was anemic, the past had to be ransacked. For both our sakes. She also needed the reminders.

What ended up being our routine? I woke up at six, cooked breakfast (something simple: she ate around twelve), went to work, called home once or twice, returned in the afternoon, cooked dinner, and talked with her if she had anything on her mind. Fears, usually. Fear of madness (*what if I lose touch with reality and remain worse than a vegetable?*), fear of abandon (*what if one day you've had enough of this and run?*), fear of suicide (*what if one day I awake to a blank in my mind and I simply go ahead?*). No true way to assuage them. Sometimes the mere act of listening seemed to work, sometimes it worsened her state. Sometimes a consolatory speech helped, sometimes it made her apprehensive. Regardless, I suspect she was without hope. What could this forty-one-year-old man possibly do that he hadn't done yet? Certainly, the pain could not be distributed. It could not be shared in any meaningful sense. And if that was not available, what then? I tried to hide the redundancy of my own lot.

I wish there was more to say about her half. It would be inspiring to speak of a struggle upward; I imagine even some kind of trajectory downward would offer relief. One just surmised the free fall. She slept, cried, and brooded, with the occasional visit to the psychiatrist added, to no real effect.

Duty and guilt. Duty and guilt. Duty and guilt.

I noticed the old tree after the makeout session of some high-schoolers. Steady amid the fever. It came to stand for many things: resignation, forbearance, impotence, quietude, lust, chastity, my wife, myself.

Then I answered. The message had been left hanging for three or four months. It was from a woman I had dated briefly after the only breakup I had with my wife early on. I had not been able to do anything about it, except masturbate to her pictures. It seemed she was married and fulfilled. But she later explained the utter isolation she felt near her husband, who year after year rejected her pleadings for sex in favor of pornography. At first, we were wary, and it showed in the inanity of our conversations; neither of us talked at length about his relationship. The fundamentals, however, emerged. We were suffocating. Once that barrier was crossed, we began to flirt.

I had to repeat to myself the reasons I didn't put a stop to it. Perhaps they would convince few people, but they convinced me. I needed an exuberant joy, one that grew from the mere presence of two bodies; I needed physical warmth, and it could all have been found by leaving my wife, but it was abundantly clear she depended on me. Thus, I held dear the concealment. I willed the duty but tired of the guilt.

Our first meeting was exceedingly awkward. I assume our exchanges had built effigies quite difficult to live up to. She faced a pale, corpulent cenobite, whereas the confident and teasing words might have suggested a bronze, brawny debauchee. I faced a hollow-eyed matron, whereas the elliptical and kinetic words actually suggested a sprightly coquette. Partial victims of make-believe. Our thirst handled the ordeal with relative ease. She seemed to take a liking to my hands,

Love—

and I grew fond of her smell. But we stuck to the surface that day.

When it all deepened, I was shaken. The clumsy ways in which we groped each other, desperate not to seem anything less than maddened, the gasping and moaning that filled the air with release, the blundering kisses that left our faces wet, evinced our drawn-out seclusion. We were a mess. And we were now equals in our strain, for I had idiotically thought my situation was grand and hers rather frivolous, unaware of the intensity of her yearning.

In this peripheral intimacy, we lost the dignified posturing of martyrdom. Pleasure disentangled our rigid dispositions, and we gained insight into our once-crumbling bodies. This time-worn piece of flesh, with its unbecoming belly and flabby limbs, exceeds the usual disgrace attached to it and now abounds in delightful memories. There is much wisdom in the psychiatrist's words.

She does not disclose much about her husband, nor am I eager to speak about my wife. These are separate lives, and we are also leaving behind the habit of amalgamation. We are many, not two. Home, I have a mind only for my wife's illness and I accommodate her needs. Outdoors, I take in the air.

The old branches spread. And I ask myself, "Can this contentment survive the tree's course as superbly as misery?"

Luna, Agueda, Lulú

I

HE OCCUPIES a minor place in my memory. In fact, were his name not mentioned again, I'm willing to bet that he'd vanish altogether. Time has nothing to do with it. I've known people who've made a difference in the space of weeks. He was just there, then he went away. I think it may have been a month. Perhaps a bit more.

I hadn't noticed him. In junior high, you only pay attention to the top and bottom of the social scale. The rest are supporting actors. All the drama I cared for came from the rejects. Though I wasn't one of them according to the divinely arbitrary sanctions of the elected, their plights, their anxieties, their fears, their triumphs were my own. As the days went by, I absorbed their whole cast. I ditched the makeup, cut my hair short, lost the bashful smile, and wore clothes loose. So I eventually joined their ranks.

These were the years of my mother's dark sunglasses. At first, I thought it was a midlife thing. She was aging. Her wrinkles were branching off. My father complained about it. Then again, I'm not sure I ever bought this. Every weekend I heard the hurried retreats, the chairs thrown against the wall, the yelling, the crying. It was really no surprise when I saw the sunglasses surrounded by a purplish mark. I stared, of course. She blamed the pillows.

I was caught off guard. Without any previous signs, he simply started talking.

"You were at the concert last night, weren't you?"
"Sorry?"
"Yeah, the teacher's band."
"Oh, right. I was."
"Kind of intimidating. The outfit, I mean."
"Ha. I guess?"

I could tell he was exhilarated. The words didn't form sentences. They rushed past in a torrent. There was something, however, lurking beneath. It seemed as if he were to suddenly overwhelm the channel. But the conversation (or rather the attempt at one) ended at a low ebb.

He then began waiting for me after classes. The way about it was feigning surprise. I'm still amused when I recall the number of times he did this. Before much had passed between us, he asked me to be his girlfriend. Though the haste was mystifying, I couldn't help sharing some of the enthusiasm. Who actually cares at that age? Besides, he was a welcome distraction.

Significantly, we met outside school once. If there is anything to cherish about our puppy love, it must be found here. I was a girl of intense habits, and I was smitten by his confessions. He hadn't kissed anyone "properly." He hadn't "really" touched anyone. So I acted as worldly as I could. We spent the whole day exploring in a park near my apartment. Amid the clumsy, hot-blooded kisses we laughed whenever we sensed a stranger staring nonchalantly. He responded to my zeal.

Luna, Agueda, Lulú

It's difficult to say how I felt. Had he left it at that, pure hormonal eagerness, there would be no ambiguity. But he didn't. He burst, as anticipated.

"Have you ever thought of suicide?"

I'll admit that in its setting it seemed an instant of great intimacy. Not only had I stumbled upon a neutral, affectionate teenager, but also an equal.

"I tried it."

"You tried thinking about it or tried doing it?"

"Doing it."

"Why?"

"I'm not sure. My life was a fucking mess. Maybe that's the reason."

"So you just went ahead?"

"Nothing special: a sharp knife. I cried for what seemed like hours before cutting my wrists. When I opened my eyes, I saw my uncle next to me. I was in the hospital. He smiled, and I was relieved. Then he sobbed."

"Are you better now?"

"I am. I won't try it again. Or if I do, I'll succeed. It was awful seeing my uncle so lost. You should meet him someday. He's gentle and funny. The only one in my family."

"Where were your parents?"

"I can't remember. Blaming each other outside? I don't know."

"I've thought about it. But it's different. Very."

"You can tell me. I just blurted everything out."

"My reasons feel silly now. They do."

"Look, we're not competing here. My life sucked and I flatlined. Other people have nice lives and they also flatline. What would be the point in shitting all over them? If you honestly want to die, fuck the skeptics."

"They're cosmic. I see no point in building a life if there's nothing afterward. I want to watch everything develop and keep on watching, enjoy and keep on enjoying."

I'll leave the rest to your imagination. They were the usual nihilistic grievances of neurotic teenagers. I listened anyway. I felt a little bit less alone. Family kept me awake, death kept him awake. We were mismatched. But we refused the role of sleepwalkers. That, I figured, was enough in common.

It wasn't. He gave excuse after excuse whenever I suggested another walk in the park. He had homework, he had to spend time with his family, he was out of the city. So I quit the shyness and told him my apartment was empty in the afternoons. I was desperate to not miss the chance of tempering my isolation. Anyway, he couldn't be bothered. He began avoiding me in recess and seemed altogether bent in pushing toward a breakup. I had to oblige.

I was puzzled, but now I have the hang of it. He had been curious about my suicide attempt long before meeting me. Apparently someone close threw that morbid detail into a conversation. He was sly. Going for a friendship would've required serious work before arriving at a confession: commitment, patience, understanding. A relationship, however, steers clear of those murky waters. Perhaps he was consoled by seeing that his life wasn't half as wrecked as mine, putting pain at the heart of his youthful tourism. Perhaps he needed sympathetic ears for once. All the same, a hideous selfishness abounds when I thumb through our stretch.

Luna, Agueda, Lulú

II

I was looking for a job as a receptionist. Since I lived for so much time as an au pair in Canada, neglecting my degree and finally burying it, the odds of landing anything related to teaching were rough. I must have been rejected by every conceivable niche in the market. The choice was not arbitrary; I had some experience working at a luxury hotel owned by an Indian multinational conglomerate. Fancy, impressive-sounding, useful in this particular interview, but otherwise a waste of my days.

He was applying for a spot in customer support. I was polite, but I confess the bafflement at seeing his appearance: his hair resembled a Stalhelm, his shirt was irregularly ironed, and his trousers were at least one size too big; the shoes were an afterthought in their very offbeat salience. After the small talk, I thought I would never see more of him. To my surprise, we were huddled into the same crowded room for training. We got to know each other better, but my attention was directed to an older graphic designer, who impossibly fought to avoid the subject of his ex-girlfriend's nymphomania, always in nostalgic tones. And I will stress the word *older*, because the graphic designer was my age, twenty-five, unlike him—a mere eighteen-year-old.

Until the breakdown, I had no glimmering of his attraction. There were plenty of girls his age. Our talks remained trivial throughout that first month. Somehow he couldn't let go of courtesy, not even in the face of raunchy humor. He did his part by laughing.

When our coach announced a reunion at her house to celebrate the end of training, I was prepared for routine work-related fun. The sight of a table struggling to retain a flood of bottles was therefore agreeable. Everyone measured time through the spillage of their drinks. I did not see him for most of the night. I was too busy with the older guy. At one point I remember seeing him enter the kitchen; I was drunk, so I thought it would be cute to give him a little kiss. Naturally, he was as drunk as I. The cutesy little kiss, then, became a short but acute clash of bodies.

We were assigned to our respective departments. Not long after, he came over to reception. His talk was, at last, lively; I made no secret of what had happened. He took it in stride, though I could see a hint of unease. He was comfortable enough, however, to stroll to my desk at least once a day. I was touched by his immaturity: he was elated to find another soul who enjoyed Plato, as if the only human beings who existed were his fifteen or seventeen acquaintances; he couldn't believe I had considered studying philosophy, as if the idea did not inhabit myriad minds, associated as it is with freedom and profoundness. I told him about a friend who was as passionate as I about these things. I agreed to introduce them.

They were not really suited to each other. My friend, a thirty-two-year-old engineer, loved the formal aspects of the discipline: mereology, the foundations of mathematics, nonmonotonic logics. He, au contraire, cared for all the big words: Truth, Reality, Virtue, Beauty. I intervened when the tension was clear. We tried this arrangement three or four times, then gave up. All along, though, his affection emboldened until we kissed again in the absence of alcohol.

He had a girlfriend. This much was clear since the beginning. I was not concerned. From my end, playfulness always prevailed. And I figured it would be the case with him. But he wondered. *Can't we do better? Why does age matter? Are you seeing someone?* No, this will do; because you know nothing of adulthood; no. I was occasionally moved. He did not hold me: he clung.

Nearing the close, he broke up with his girlfriend. With a less charming immaturity, he asked more of our days. The nights spent loitering, laughing, and loving little sufficed. He was not stupid: I was left to infer disappointment through the help of offhand remarks. A disappointment bred from the expectation of immediate certainty, of immediate relief, pledge, insurance. But I would refuse explicitly and as many times as needed.

Maybe a year had gone by when he quit. As usual, he approached my desk. His talk was flat and courteous again, with a trifle of hardness adhering to arbitrary parts of his speech. Innocuous memories were scavenged. Vague plans years into the hypothetical future known to all former comrades were made. Anything but affection. He must have resumed his relationship. I wouldn't know. He cut me off from his life, as if the stray weed added nothing to the beauty of the garden.

III

We exchanged furtive glances in class, aware of an underlying sense of complicity. I was fond of his theatrics. They seemed to flow from a genuine love for his subject. He could not help plunging into vast and elaborate digressions whenever a name or technical term pointed in another direction. It was usually the awkward laugh of a student at the end of a cumbersome sentence that made him conscious of the need to retrace his steps. Those were some of the few moments in which you could notice embarrassment in his demeanor. Apart from that, he was all confidence.

I had no intention of talking to him after class even though he appeared close to my age. I was seeing someone then, a vibrant boy who'd done his best to open me up to teeming life. But the frequent contact with this garrulous type was estranging me. I thought frequently of what a convenient instant to draw near would look like. It came when in one of his outpourings he grazed the matter of photography: the gist of it was eerily similar to an esteemed cousin's reflections. I said as much, and he showed interest. From then on, we would have brief give-and-takes before his next class.

Addicted as we both were to these interludes, I decided to multiply them by waiting for another pause. When he saw me, headphones snuffing out my singing, he seemed gratified. I was disappointed. The reaction I was going for carried much more warmth. His smirk, with all its connotations of wise prediction, irritated me. This talk was unbalanced and constrained by an air of sufficiency. We left school and were about to part ways in a somewhat frigid manner. At the last minute, however, he briskly rested his hand on my waist.

I began avoiding his eyes. His discourses were not lofty anymore, but rather facile and superficial. I initially dreaded the end of class. Would he act as sure as ever? Would he make a cynical comment? Would he explain himself? None, apparently. He maintained his distance. There was an inertia that hoped for the habitual pleasantries when the moment to leave sneaked up. I relented only when the idea occurred to me to put him in his place.

He was as before. I wondered whether he would like to go for a walk one Saturday afternoon. He would. We set the date and time. When the day arrived, I went into bed, cozied up, and gloated over this minor but definite statement.

I imagined he would again lapse into distance. Prideful as he always looked, he wished to reschedule. He understood. This was so far the greatest acknowledgement he had made. I was tempted to decline. His repentant expression was on the verge of cracking. But I did want to know more about him.

He was twenty-three years old, not out there enough to disprove my guess. His brash bearing diminished little, yet it fell sufficiently short of that unnerving pitch which had exasperated me. We were quick to probe into each other's lives. I listed my boyfriend's labors to enliven all around him—my mother's unique brand of solipsism, which permitted a constant pestering of her daughters—my father's sophisticated tyranny and its high-minded demands, all within the bounds of reason. He, on the other hand, stuck with a curiously minute issue: his addiction to bricolage. He explained how to chase an illumination he would sacrifice any adjustment to facts, he would make use of every prompt, every omen, struggling and even suffocating in the labyrinth of haphazard associations, ignorant of his future self's priggish regrets. He had fun, and that was that—he endured the strictures.

As the seams became evident, my attachment expanded. He acted as if no vulnerabilities had been exposed by his confessions, but I'm certain this was a way of asking for me to play along. I did so with sympathy. I learned to care in spite of the risk.

I don't believe I lie when I say that my boyfriend meant a good deal to me. But he was far more complete than I. That is, he no longer remembered what it was like to feel utterly at a loss, quite fretful. I needed someone who could be by my side in a stricter sense, who could wonder at what I wondered and fear what I feared. Or, at least, who could give an answer other than *it is to be expected*.

He was not going to be it. He cleared any doubts in a thoroughly unnatural, tense, frivolous conversation.

"I am not interested. I've just left one."

"Then I'm not interested in anything else."

"Fine with me. I am not going to be tied through these ultimatums."

"What are you going on about? Ultimatums? Wanting to be with you?"

"You can reframe it. But I find nothing of value in attaching a label."

"I do. If you don't care, then let it go. It'll be the same for you."

"This is ridiculous. Pure convention."

"Get over it already."

"No. It makes no sense. Let's leave things here if it's so crucial."

"Great."

We were remarkably of a piece. So much so that he later confessed to melancholy. By then he was an anecdote that could be shared in evenings of mild heartbreak, one forgotten with the sip of a coffee and the snugness of a blanket.

Bloom

HE SPEAKS as if I cared the least bit about English usage. He lets no sentence go without some form of emendation. By fits and starts, he recounts a vivid childhood betrayal. There is a grasping for elegance, correctness, which contrasts with the boorish movements of his body. As my mind gallivants, the suspicion overcomes me that he might be recounting a bar fight. His knee strikes my left buttock every time he needs to emphasize the intensity of a particular feeling. I let out a faint laugh when the sudden brush of my breasts arouses him. Politely annoyed, he resumes his story. His eyes, however, drift. As is clear, our momentous passion nears its natural end.

We fall asleep after a difficult second time. He has trouble keeping an erection. I assure him that it is a light matter, but the neurotic in him resents me in the morning (politely, yes). It's an easy shot: if I were sincere, I would beg him to fuck me before we leave the bed. This hard-boiled obsession with desire is typical of a rising sense of ownership. We pass breakfast in silence. And that's the way it goes.

I have a stable job and a magnificent routine. Everything must be in its place before I spend my afternoons looking for a spark. I am, to be sure, addicted to beginnings. There is no room in my body for the accommodation of lukewarm familiarity. And I speak in the most general terms. The thing is, I am as realistic as possible. I know I must cede in almost all parts of my life; otherwise, I would be heading southward. So I maintain my translations impeccable though I scoff at the dullness of every page, I'm agreeable to my colleagues though they bore me to death, I read edifying, up-to-the-minute books though I yawn at the authors' unfaltering self-importance, and I exercise six days a week though I loathe the vengeful atmosphere of gyms. But it's worth it. The bridled emotions burgeon when it's time to surface.

Knowing someone who calls forth a distinct part of you is unmatched. And it is easy to see when there will be variation. The bland workaholic exercises the facade, the expansive crusader transmits his delirium, the pouty bohemian bolsters some whims, the guilt-ridden novice feeds tenderness, the neurotic intellectual asks for ripostes, the extravagant dandy enlivens the adornments, the labored Don Juan offers lustful calisthenics, and the authoritative brat unloads the mind. I'm being unfair, however. They are alike if one is on the lookout for obvious similarities. Sure, the Don Juans push and pull, strive to make themselves mysterious, but they have unique backgrounds from which they acquire touching tics. In the end, when ardor takes possession, we all want to please.

Until we don't. And the last flicker makes itself known through a thin halo. That's when you see a distinctive person become a biological construct. At least nowadays. Perhaps in other times they became a theological construct or a mechanical one. Whatever. The point is the shedding of idiosyncrasy. I don't care much about the bohemian gently preaching his flight from convention, but I do care when I no longer listen to his fumbling sweet talk (so filtered through his character) and instead have to deal with his jealous epiphanies.

There is a pattern. First, what once was blatant pleasure, now betrays possibilities. Could this ecstatic moan reach a higher pitch? Could this shivering approach the uproar of convulsion? Secondly, conjectures spring up. Maybe a bigger cock would do? Maybe a beastly endurance would help? Thirdly, a mythical man is outlined. He has everything that the fantasizer lacks or possesses in a lesser degree. Lastly, an acquaintance embodies the myth. The mere name conjures an image of voluptuous abandon. And then comes the need for reassurance.

It is all very dramatic and wearisome. I've let myself get carried away two or three times. Hopeful. But there's nothing pleasant at the other end. This jealousy marks the middle. If confidence is regained, what was lost will return only in isolated episodes. The rest is a subtle and cumulative withdrawal.

I understand the need to embellish this. Where would we be were people to face the dearth of genuine desire? So I've grown accustomed to the platitudes. Uncontrollable magnetism between bodies pales in the presence of rarefied affection: look at them oblivious to their nudity, so above it that a decorous kiss on the cheek is enough. Oh, yes! Their love has reached the heavens. They can now neglect their shells and sneer at the shallowness of youth, or at the baseness of adults who still hunger for zest.

But the platitudes acquire intensity with each passing year. At forty-five, I am made aware that sex is to be increasingly discarded in favor of a folksy quietism. A given for married women. Or if not a given, an expectation that can be met with relative ease. You already have the conditions set: an exhausted mate, demanding children, and an imaginary though forceful boundary. In my case, it is a touch more nauseating. Now it is rare for my relationships to begin with the view of a bridge. There is a damning offer at the outset: take the stairs; that is, start from the middle. Be it a man of thirty or of fifty, the eyes are telling. *You're past your prime, my dear, you have no leverage.* They do. They are the ones who have an eternal blessing to fuck. The cock doesn't age, does it? So long as it's able to stand, it is catered to. Of course, age considerably diminishes desire here also; it can breed condescension. But what of the cunt? It has its moment, and then the curtain is lowered amid whistles and applause. If anyone dare raise it, there is no condescension: you'll have to deal with outrage and disgust. The cunt after a certain decade can be talked about only as an object of nostalgia.

A predicament to love beginnings, then. We middle-aged ladies must know better and secretly hanker for the golden days, when our faces were silken, our breasts firm, and our asses pert. We'll see our albums feigning interest in the events, but deep down we'll envy our own distant bodies. And this'll all grow keener for the coming generations, so engrossed in the miracle of their image.

Or we can finish burying creeds that are already comfortable in the grave. There's resistance, sometimes excessively so, but when one follows the direction of an incontestable tendency, one from which flows the ebullience of life, it is outclassed.

He stops at the door and seems hesitant. He turns to me.

"I'd like to hear a childhood story from you. Dinner at nine?"

I nod. To my delight, I still err in placing the transition.

Loneliness by the Window

MOROSE AND TACITURN, she responded to the howls of twenty-year-olds and teenagers in three-word sentences that hardly demanded a full breath. Some of them delighted in the acknowledgement and went their own way, laughing and hitting the brave soul who took the chance; others were struck silent, and slowly tried to amend their gaffe with an attempt at actual conversation; not a few shouted all the forms in which they wished to fuck her if only she asked for it or gave the slightest hint, performing the act with an imaginary girl while their pals rallied them on. With the second she had something of a friendship.

It was regular by then for her to lean out of the apartment window in the afternoons. As soon as she woke up, she had to take care of her four-year-old sister and help her fourteen-year-old brother get ready for work. There was no venturing outside; her father had long ago been jailed and her mother headed to another state in order to work for a cousin. She sent money, but not nearly enough for a passable life. At sixteen, Soledad was justifiably a cynic.

I had to sneak out to meet with her. My parents reminded me every time they could that there are some people on this blessed earth who, try as they might, would not amount to anything given their circumstances. Far be it from us to lend a hand and waste valuable energy that could advance our own difficult placement. But I kept at it. The excuses were plentiful, since I excelled in my studies.

She was two years older. At fourteen, however, the difference is profound. I was there mostly to listen. The things I could talk about were inert in her day-to-day. There were three subjects: family, the howlers downstairs, and drugs. Her tone was lighthearted when she spoke about her little sister, then grew bitter when naming her mother or brother; to Soledad, they were two sides of the same improvident coin—mediocre, coarse spendthrifts. One sent unpredictable amounts of money, while the other had to be admonished to keep any amount at hand. *We have to eat, Rodrigo.* Or some such variation. Turning to the howlers and the drugs they occasionally provided, she changed her tone to one of worldliness. My virginity was unbecoming, and the fact that I didn't smoke or drink evidenced a sheltered little ingénue, not a woman. I was careful not to go over whenever I could hear all the whistling and swearing. Yet I eventually met some of the guys. They were as loud and as forthright as I imagined. They talked about my long pale legs, my long straight hair, all the while making sure I caught the overtones. Soledad tried to assure me with scornful grimaces. *Leave them be, they're not the worst of them.* After the noise, they settled on more serious matters—the shit pay they received from men devoted to the morals of their community, the abusive older colleagues who considered it a duty to perpetuate the humiliations of the pecking order, the resigned mother who always told them that one must first roll in the mud to be worthy of the upper echelon, the dignified father who insisted that even if painful work came to nothing the struggle still mattered because the mud had its inherent merit, and the brothers and sisters who lacked nerve and derailed into a life of petty crimes that kept the family on edge when a stranger approached the doorstep. And Soledad had advice to spare. *Go spray his never-to-be-paid Oldsmobile. Tell all of them to shove it up their already loose behinds. Fuck her pious, half-assed, dead advice. The pop can suck a fitting, righteous cock. Let them taste the end of that particular swallow.* It seemed I was the only one aware of the irony. But the language relieved, at least momentarily, their burdens. They left empowered, and she looked proud. I couldn't make out whether this intervention was common, since it was the last time I got to see them.

Soledad cleaned house when Orondo, a psychologist, moved to her apartment complex. He was a portly middle-aged man who corrected you briskly if you didn't address him as *doctor*, eager to point out that few gentlemen in this world attained such high distinction. *Let us count our blessings*. In a matter of days he made the acquaintance of everyone in the building. Most, if not all, of the community was charmed by his antiquated manners and emphatic tone. Moreover, he had a knack for scolding the youth in imperious jeremiads. For the men, he reserved one list of moral faults (torpidity, exuberance, churlishness) and for the women another (nympholepsy, vanity, boldness). In time, I was the recipient owing to a short skirt I had barely mustered the courage to wear.

"To think that a beautiful young woman as yourself would seek the approval of hot-headed boys by demeaning her self-image, by twisting it into a foreign fantasy, by abandoning that quiet, blissful ignorance which makes a thorough happiness, the only one, in this otherwise nefarious journey. Truly, I beseech you to be your authentic self and leave this tainted spectacle to those who know no better. Open your eyes. Open them! Life as yet hasn't pronounced her ineluctable sentence and still ruminates upon your proper place."

And, with this bombast left behind, he buttoned the middle of his shirt, threw back a thin stray hair that had stuck to his forehead, and bowed awkwardly, paying little attention to my panicked face.

If it hadn't been for my pouring of emotions that day, Soledad would've probably postponed any talk about Orondo. I really wanted to hear her excoriate the brazenness of this stranger, I wanted her to be as explicit as ever; instead, she explained the good heart behind the harsh words.

"You know how old guys act, Regina. They have this idea that they have been sent into the world to protect the young ones."

"What a creep! Seriously. I didn't even register him. What's his business looking after my outfit? I can't tell you how embarrassing it was. You remember how self-conscious I've been with skirts and shorts and all that stuff. And when I have the guts, here comes this old *pervert* and starts going on and on and on about it."

"Pervert? Come on. Don't be such a brat. He thought he was doing you a favor."

"Are you actually saying this? You? The woman that's experienced a lifetime of sleazy comments?"

"Mostly from stupid kids. Oro's not a kid. He's old-school."

Oro. That's how people began calling him. I think I first heard it from Soledad. In any case, it was a term of endearment. She had clearly spoken with him beyond what could be called polite. But she insisted it was not the case. Mere neighbors, mere small talk. Yet where were the howlers? Not only did she cease letting them into the apartment, but she also ceased letting them gather outside. Her justification was the need for a change of air. She needed "people" around her that would contribute something of substance. All this talk of moral self-improvement reeked of Orondo's sweaty philosophy. But I hadn't seen them together, and when he would cross paths with us, he was perfectly antediluvian in his motions. Not a trace of warmth.

Orondo's formerly decorative role in the community started to acquire a different hue. He now spent his afternoons giving out free lunches to the children and teenagers who played outside the building and sharing the leftovers with the vagrants who loafed around the block. This last act brought him a couple of complaints, to which he responded in his usual vein.

"Fear not the accrual of this sorry batch! They are weak, they are amnesiac, they are in the throes of insanity. They have no thought for our petty speculations. And they are, heaven knows, as human as we are. Why spread thin an already meager piece of bread? Leave it be, leave it be."

And it seemed this ran parallel to his involvement with Soledad. As always, she leaned out her apartment window, but the howlers were long gone, and in their place was civic Orondo. He asked about her brother, her sister, her parents. Predictably, he had lessons to impart; she would stare with amusement and something else akin to affection. I couldn't help objecting to the development of this strange bond. I feared our friendship would strain, but Soledad's erstwhile worldly condescension transformed into a motherly conceit, which preserved her sympathy at the cost of leaving my words powerless—the words of her sheltered little ingénue.

In one of my mercurial moods, I retreated. Orondo had become too much the center of people's lives, too much the center of Soledad's life. It was no good. Hadn't they all protested against the pushy politicians who came every campaign season with truckloads of provisions, only to disappear without any meaningful interaction? How was Orondo any different? As far as I knew, he wasn't close to anyone, he kept fellowship on the surface. Besides, his qualifications were as suspect as those of your typical politician. Yes, he may have studied sociology, but where was the knowledge? Yes, Orondo may have studied psychology, but where were his insights? He was on the same wavelength as my father, even if his language was a bit more pompous. But word about him reached me for most of my withdrawal. My mother was friends with one of the building's tenants, a very old lady who lived with her twelve-year-old grandson. Apparently, Orondo was giving therapy at a price left to the patient's goodwill. His earnings were spent on maintenance costs and on the education of the poorest tenants' children. Soledad didn't have to linger much before my mind, since the old lady eventually spoke of Orondo's *mistress*, an underage girl who had been living by herself for years. To be sure, the old lady raised doubts about that status, and insisted Orondo would never encroach upon anyone's innocence. Afterward, my mother inquired whether this underage girl could be Soledad.

"I can't say. We haven't seen each other in a while."

"Oh. I hope she is. It would do wonders for her life to have the guidance of someone as educated as this Oro everyone's raving about."

"Orondo. I mean, wow, you worried about me going over to her place, but you don't care that a sixty-year-old man is dating her?"

"Oh, don't be silly, Regina. It is pure gossip. Even here, where people are less prone to misbehave, the rumor went out that your father had a *very* young mistress."

"How would you know it's just a rumor?"

"Your father is a busy man. And so is this Oro . . . Orondo. Sounds like he has too many things going on."

"Maybe he's doing everything to catch her attention."

"Ah, of course. I sometimes forget I'm speaking with a teenager. Only a fourteen-year-old would figure all actions in someone's life can revolve around a single person."

And with this fairly common put-down, my mother resumed her activities, leaving me agitated. Was I misjudging this in-your-face Samaritan? Did his theatrical rage and formality spring from good faith? Was he candidly outdated? Although then and there I felt an urge to meet with Soledad, I waited. I was too restive.

I had been intimidated by Orondo's reprimand. So much so that I had worn only jeans or long skirts when visiting Soledad. After the respite, however, I wore the original skirt and even added the high heels with which my mother struggled to walk straight. Orondo was painting the grill that covered the building's electric meters. He looked at me and shook his head with impatience.

"I see. You wish for approval of your recklessness. Or you wish for outrage. I am afraid you will find none here. In the depths of your conscience something will come of it."

I tried to grin, though a grimace must have welcomed his comment, since he sighed and went back to work. As I took the stairs, his voice bellowed in a singularly incensed tone.

"No, no, no. Soledad is not home. She has renounced her lassitude. Now her afternoons are spent elsewhere. If you desire to communicate something of weight, please feel free to address me."

"I simply wanted to talk with her."

"Prattle, is it? Soledad has no more time for it."

"Are you serious?"

"I am, indeed, serious. She has shared her thoughts about you. Do not think I ignore your doubts or, for that matter, your type."

"What? What do you care about us? Who are you, anyway?"

"*Us*. You are partially correct. I do not care for you. You do not belong here. You belong with your snail-paced ilk over there."

As he said this, he grabbed a stone and threw it toward the avenue that separated my neighborhood from Soledad's.

"Have you ever cared about your *friend*? Have you done anything other than rebelling against your parents to see her, a dejected girl who dwindled into nothing seeking consolation in nympholepsy and nostrums? You are a mere spectator, a tourist who slumbers peacefully, in the knowledge that the slums alone can gratify the hunger for picturesque settings, all along making light of the *friend* who has to see after two underfed siblings."

I had trouble centering on the details. I could pick up only the vague accusation that I hadn't done anything for Soledad. I turned my back to him and hurried home. After crossing the avenue, I tripped. I hadn't been aware of how much my legs had been shaking. I was on the verge of tears, but an involuntary exhalation burst forth an overpowering feeling of anger. I grabbed my heels, headed backward,

Loneliness by the Window

and threw them in Orondo's direction. I was tempted to curse my way into his head, to make him slightly conscious of the repulsion I felt for him, to leave clear that not everyone admired him, that there was at least one person who knew he was fundamentally insincere. But my voice didn't come through. And Orondo stood there, glancing at the heels with an air of consequence.

It was thanks to Soledad's brother, who had left his job and was now able to study, that I knew of her whereabouts. She worked at a grocery store, two miles from her apartment. Orondo had told her that working for her family would give her the edification she needed. Moreover, it would allow her to cut ties with her mother. Soledad would not be in a position to object, since he even offered to take care of her little sister. Though her brother had no strong opinion regarding the move, I did—it seemed to be another step toward isolating her.

Our late encounter was significant. For most of the time I knew her, I had refused to believe there was any barrier between us, excepting, of course, my lack of experience (which could have easily been overcome). And it had looked that way from her side also. She had implied as much in her invitations and all-around sororal attitude. As I approached her, however, she appeared bent on dismissing everything.

"What's happening? Where have you been? I had to reach out to your brother to get in touch with you."

"That should've given you a clue."

"Soledad, what's the matter? You're suddenly taking orders from this guy?"

"Oro's done nothing but good. Are you still that up your own ass? He's right, you know. It's all been make-believe to you."

"Oh my god. Really? You're giving more weight to his fucking tiresome rants?"

"I'm giving more weight to his actions. Did you know he takes care of my sister? Did you know he's helping my brother get through school? Did you know he's preparing me for high school? You don't, and that's the point."

"Soledad, come on! We're not adults. We can't be crucified for not understanding how to do things, right? I've always been here for you. I mean it. Now that I know how it all goes I can do my part. We don't need some tyrant to kick us around."

"You keep saying *we*. Maybe *you* can experiment and pick up where *you* left off. I can't. My brother and sister can't. Go lend a hand to people who have your time."

"You're just doing your best to push me away. Are you with him?"

By then, her exasperation was obvious. She refused to say another word, and I could not bring myself to stop pleading. I had other friends, but with none of them could I breathe the air I had breathed with her. I had cherished her rawness, even if unsustainable; her nonconformity, even if puerile; her resourcefulness, even if hamstrung. And I trusted we could figure something out on our own.

But Orondo had the supreme advantage of unquestioned expertise. What could anyone possibly say to one who outranked them all? He had the civilizing blueprint laid out in his mind—it was a matter of following his orders. What could a teenager possibly say if he pressed for a symbolic gift from his community?

As I saw Soledad greet Orondo, who now occupied the window in regal fashion, I finally felt an exile.

Confessions of an American Marihuana User

To the Reader

WOULD YOU NOT AGREE, dear reader, that ours is an age of prejudice? When the freedom that we all praise descends from the fog of abstraction and stares at us in its chilling concreteness, do we not shudder? Indeed, our rampant hedonism fetters us to our little pleasures and narrows our view. It gives us what seems to be the only warmth available to our fragmented consciousness. And thus the world becomes a pitiful stimulus that has to wage war with all its denials. A person of science? Rather a person of some meager, arcane patch of science. A philosopher? Rather a dryasdust soul that dabbles in the limits of sense. An artist? Rather a coddled charlatan that thinks their inner voice the universe: one sentence, a star cluster. A believer? Rather a banal Candide. An entrepreneur? Rather the punching bag of technocrats. We must rebel against these molds. And the path lies in confronting the highest and the lowest that our experiences have to offer, in confronting that we have always been broken.

I propose to begin with a subject that might appear the antipode of loftiness—marihuana. Even at present the word is an unwelcome guest. We have two sides and two sides only: that of the *potheads* and that of the *tietwats*. I, who have had my stay with both, wish to call attention to a true middle position: what the majority regards as the middle is merely indifference. I have experienced in no uncertain terms the abysses and the raptures of this old drug. I must also add, without breach of truth or modesty, that my constitution is particularly suited for this endeavor. I am one of those persons who, as Hume put it, "are subject to a certain *delicacy* of *passion*, which makes them extremely sensible to all the accidents of life."

Yet to dive immediately into the topic would be a blunder. The background of a life is needed. Drugs, in all their varieties, shuffle the sceneries of memory with the technique of a cardsharp. It is difficult, almost impossible, to account for the erratic behaviors that emerge if this is brushed aside. Count on it that the happy drunk has in him a robust source of joy, bought at a cheap price when young! Ponder the fact that the raging reefer-freak has in him a wasteland, panhandled in successive tragedies!

Prelusive

How does one end with a joint in one's hands? Is it through a series of awkward interactions, oddly similar to those that take place in your typical tietwat PSA? Or is it through an estimable pal who just wants to have a good time? In my case, there was pathos involved. I ran toward it seeking shelter from a long-lasting melancholia.

My father was a benign alcoholic. As an illegal immigrant, his prospects were abject. And it was expected that he should accept them with stern dignity.

To complain was to be ungrateful and invite a humbling. His life until then had been worse than any requirement. He carried the weight. Eventually, he met my mother. She admired his character and somehow transformed admiration into a tepid love. But since the beginning she could not stand my father's time-honored solace. The sheepish smile that often gave him away soured when she stonewalled him. He simply went outside, adjusted his folding chair, and stared the rest of the night at the cats that had an inordinate fondness for our garden.

My mother, an august and somber woman, grew bitter. The perfect excuse presented itself when my father took one of the cats by the tail and violently threw it against the neighbors' car. It was an unexplainable act of rage. Even now I cannot account for it. We packed our belongings and left in less than a week.

What a futile thing to assign blame! My father was a victim of habit, my mother a victim of expectations. I have never felt above them. I was eleven when it all collapsed. Afterward, life moved on without an excess of disarray. And there was one gift for which I will always be grateful to my father: my knowledge of Spanish. By the time I had classes, my command of that language was so great that I could read Cervantes, Góngora, and Quevedo, and point out their solecisms. Naturally, my father had no academic interest in his native tongue. Therefore, his Spanish was rich in idioms and racy of the soil. This is the golden entrance. Unfortunately for me, my professors were dullards. How did they expect me to show interest if their knowledge was confined to a couple of model verbs and a stuffed vocabulary?

In any case, some of them understood the chasm and let me read during their class. At this moment, I came under the spell of that titan of Modernismo—Juan Ramón Jiménez. It was through his influence that the vague emotions I had been feeling then acquired a diaphanous quality. I remember the exact day one of his *Arias* revealed the sight of my misery. I was at a bus stop, delaying my arrival home. The words seemed overheard.

> En el jardín cantan: oigo
> gritos, palabras y risas;
> la casa está silenciosa,
> toda ha quedado vacía.

Delight dwelt outside.

> Sólo yo, triste y rendido,
> sueño visiones fatídicas
> en este balcón que guarda
> besos, lágrimas y risas.

And I, inscrutably fatigued, remained on the balcony.

An uncaused melancholy drives one to despair, for one knows not where to direct one's efforts. I was falling. Nonetheless, sharing this newfound awareness was out of the question. My mother struggled to keep us going—I had to do my part.

Vitam continet una dies.[1] I woke up, already worn out, asked myself why I should prepare for the day, and marched on, ignoring the obvious answer. The orbit of my thoughts had the clichéd nihilistic rants as its focus. Only the occasional poem distracted me, since I was also profoundly alone. I had friends, but their blithe babbling and stentorian laughs aggravated my

---

[1] The parallels with Johnson's period of despondency do not escape me.

proneness to daydreaming. I was not really there with them. I was elsewhere. *Sólo yo, triste y rendido.*

I had a dim hope that my melancholy would come to an end. Thus I did not entertain the possibility that it would go on indefinitely, transforming my life into a gray blot. Suicide may appear enticing to the majority. Yet, as I said before, my constitution is delicately tuned. Certainly, the idea of closing one's eyes forever, resting at last, was not easily shunned. That was one extreme. The other: life. Even at the bottom I could not help wondering at the miracle that is the movement of my limbs and the ceaseless stream of my brain. Wonderful, indeed, be it the product of chance or of a steady hand.

But do not think I had any heroic spirit. When time came to register for college, I knew it would be a short-lived affair. My mother, however, once more constructed an elaborate future on the ruins of somebody else. I refuse to detail these days. It is dispiriting to admit that they were perhaps my mother's happiest. Suffice it to say that when I broke the news of desertion, I lost her. I can only imagine: years of toil for one who is as adrift as you.

I left home close to my nineteenth birthday. I was able to rent a small room with my savings, but they could not last for more than two months. I dreaded the idea of a job. Not out of laziness, of course. I was not blind to the poor opportunities a dropout would have.

As the end of the first month approached, my relationship with the tenant developed. She was a phlegmatic woman of thirty who worked at a call center. I had no intention of socializing, yet there was something in her manner that made me feel less dejected. Every night, when she arrived from work, she offered a cup of coffee and then sat down to read a book—not any type of book, mind you: the *Zibaldone*.[2] It was a peculiar routine. She did not talk to me; she simply gave me the coffee and pored over the pages. At first, I immediately went to my room; later on, owing to a gracious "you can stay if you like," I remained a bit longer. She maintained her silence. But the routine was placid.

One evening in which I was not particularly down, I asked her about the book. She said she bought it at a second-hand bookstore. She was not familiar with the author; she bought it out of mere curiosity. And she liked it.

"I have felt tempted to skip some pages, but I don't know . . . I find that disrespectful. If I ever wrote about something I loved, I would like for people to give it a chance. Even if it's Greek or Latin."

I transcribe these words because I have a superstition. I believe that at some moment in life we enunciate a couple of sentences that epitomize us. I was lucky enough to witness hers. It would become clear that even the ellipsis played its part.

When the second month concluded, I explained my situation. She already knew about my proficiency in Spanish. As a result, she offered to wait for me to get a job related to it. She insisted I could avoid exploitation. This marked the beginning of a predictably anemic pilgrimage. I cannot remember the number of doors I knocked, the number of aseptic rooms I entered, the number of deceptive questions I was asked, the number of hackneyed mission statements I had to endure, in sum, the number of times I had to show a submissive attitude. All for the greater good of living hand-to-mouth.

---

[2]This book may strike readers as convenient, but I hope charity will let them see that we have always learned our lessons in narrative from the beautiful coincidences of life itself.

I landed a job at a shoddy nursing school. They knew my background was lacking. Nevertheless, sacrifices had to be made for the sake of curriculum diversity. Students were aware of my symbolic presence and reacted with appropriate respect for tradition—they sunk into apathy.

I still wonder at my ability to go on. Yet I would be conceited if I denied the tenant's share. For, not to remind my fellow Hispanists of the old Spanish proverb, *Quien a buen árbol se arrima*, she staved off my utter defeat with her coffees and terse conversations. When a basic structure is laid down, time rushes. I was no exception.

And now, having given a brief account of my life and the latter-day hound, I address the remedy.

The Raptures of Use

There is a certain foolishness to the idea of a pioneer. We are all secretly indebted. The only true pioneers have been engulfed by the time before time. Thus I have countless illustrious predecessors. But I feel compelled to single out just one: Ludlow, the hasheesh eater. This unfairly obscure man had a flair for introspection, and were it not for the impossibly bountiful worlds open to our souls and constitutions, his words would be definitive. Therefore, I will commence with one of his captivating images.

"If the disembodied ever return to hover over the hearth-stone which once had a seat for them, they look upon their friends as I then looked upon mine." There you have *le mot juste*: "disembodied." If I had to emphasize the sum of marihuana's effects, I would choose that one word. In it the spectrum of joy and grief finds a proper outlet, for we human beings are capricious creatures, never really at ease with the stubborn dualism of mind and body. Let me turn, then, to joy.

It was through a friend of the tenant's that I became acquainted with marihuana. After a particularly worthless day at work, I arrived home to a party of three. The first thing that struck me was the pungent smell. Then I noticed a man of about forty reading passages from the *Zibaldone* to the tenant and a woman her age. They were both huddled in a corner, giggling and murmuring, while the man coughed and stared in wonder at the pages.

"Ah! This guy was twenty years old? Genius!"

"I think . . . I mean, I think I get where he's coming from."

"Yeah, yeah. Life's a government project without funding."

All their comments were full of arbitrary inflections. I stood for a while near the door, hesitating to join. They acted as if I had not recently entered. Perhaps ten minutes passed before the man looked in my direction, squinting as if I were miles away. I was still unsure whether it would be worthwhile to stay with them, but they were quite friendly. When they offered a joint, I refused on the grounds that I was burnt up. I had no real reason to try it. At that time, I was indifferent toward drugs. The middle-aged man smiled.

"Hey, no judging. And look, I know it's none of my business, but your friend here told me about your depression. Give this a try someday. It isn't magic. Well, it kind of is, but it can help you gain perspective. This and young Leopardini."

They all laughed uncontrollably, as if this rather innocuous comment were a full-fledged joke. I went over to my room not long after. Yet I weighed the words of the jocund man for the rest of the night.

I decided to ask the tenant for the drug. She was ambivalent.

"You shouldn't make too much of what Harold said. He acts as if marihuana were a panacea. If you insist, sure, I can give you some. But I repeat: do not deposit all your hopes in it. What's more, be prudent and start slow. I suggest you take it while I'm here, in case you need anything."

The warning, back then, seemed misplaced.

It was a Sunday the tenant was not home that I began smoking. I was in my room, staring at the ceiling. Within minutes, I felt a curious buzz in my head. Initially, I thought this was owing to mere suggestion. But I did not have to wait much before the buzz traveled through my body. It was as if it were gently releasing my mind from the now numb flesh. Free in this unusual way, consciousness raced from one half-formed image to another, content with leaving behind exquisite outlines of the whole that embraced them. The speed blurred that other outline called "I." Overwhelmed by the number of associations that offered themselves promiscuously, I glanced at the clock and cracked up. Ten minutes had elapsed, not the imagined hour. And so it was, reader, that time ushered its ridiculous child, at last scornful of the walker of matter, into a lavish garden, where he could romp at leisure and forget himself.

In due course, still in a quixotic trance, I stood and looked for a mirror. Like Prado, I was seized by a crisis of laughter. What a silly thing it was to exist in such a limited mode. I regarded the reflection with pity. Soon, I fell asleep.

Melancholy continued, but at least now I could pause it. Is it surprising that I started frequenting the middle-aged man? He introduced me to the halcyon counterpart of our world. Music unveiled its concealed tempo, Painting flaunted its transporting gorgeousness, Cinema disclosed its Ovidian overtones. The city, otherwise bland, became a tenuous fog through which I hovered. For the time being, my mind was untethered to commonplace perception. More importantly, I saw myself from afar. Oh, Protean plant, to all souls alike you offer the shade of distance! To all you whisper the gospel of detachment! But will you ever reveal completely the spectacle above the spectacle? Will you let this prison of finitude grasp it untainted? Mercurial plant! *Terra incognita*! Who is to be your Cortés? And will he have his own *Noche Triste* as a spur? Or are you an intractable Ocean that will forever refuse conquest? This I know—you are proof of our parochial cast, of our lack of grit, of our frailty. You are an artful confrontation!

Introduction to the Abysses of Use

In my state, it was increasingly difficult to resist the lure of daily consumption and larger doses. And to this the middle-aged man had a solution: edibles. Before I go on, it would be prudent to assert the obvious: he was a self-described pothead, a label he found benign. I can assure the perplexed reader it certainly is not. For it encloses those who believe themselves the devotees of a gentle religion—and an infallible one, as is usual. Thus they proselytize with a rarely seen fervor.[3] They blame the people and never that which occupies the

---

[3] The reader will not ignore the prevalent frigid draft that wanders through the halls of the Catholic Church. I have long suspected that in these new popular religions one can find the former heat.

pedestal. Theirs is a do-it-yourself theology that discredits chance and restores the infallible will. Like countless clay figurines, they stand blind, mute, and deaf to suffering. Let me turn, then, to grief.

The Abysses of Use

> La verdad es una brújula loca que no funciona en este caos de cosas desconocidas.
>
> Pío Baroja, *El árbol de la ciencia*

Eating marihuana is in every important sense different from smoking it. The act is more intimate; the arrival of the high is slower. The experience acquires an altogether novel savor. It took me no time to prefer this method. And I could not wish for a better situation. The middle-aged man had a continuous batch of pastries.

Up until then, I had been relatively free from unpleasant episodes. Here and there I had reached a disagreeable awareness of a lurking anxiety, but not much else. I became as brash a consumer as my dealer.

The eclipse of sanity emerged without warning.

I was at one of the middle-aged man's home reunions. The tenant usually gave an excuse not to go. Reasonable, I thought. In the center of the kitchen, there was an old yellow tray brimming with brownies. All pieces had been carefully and symmetrically cut. I ate one and sat down to wait for the effect. Maybe half an hour later, a lanky fellow approached me and began chatting away. He was clearly stoned. What he said is of no importance: I can hardly remember. My body was by then twitching uncontrollably. At some point, I tried looking at his eyes to tell him to leave me be. But before I could say a word, an orange spiral formed in his chin. This I had never seen. I went to the bathroom sink and splashed water on my face, cautious of the mirror. I took a deep breath and gazed at the living room. Somehow I felt it was not good for me to be there. Among the multitude, I could catch a pair of cagey eyes. I started pacing, telling myself this was to be expected: drugs are unpredictable. I had not realized my mouth was absurdly dry. But I did not drink anything. Too much was happening at the same time. Suddenly, I was sitting on the couch. I had no recollection of my movement. Then I was reclining against a wall. Then I was grabbing a chair in the kitchen for support. It seemed that every blink transported me to a new scenario. I was frightened by this lack of control. As my eyes wandered in the living room, I stopped breathing. Or so I thought. I tried to breathe again. My fear increased a thousandfold when I came to believe I would have to attend to this simple act deliberately for the rest of my life. I was lost. And my break with reality was just beginning. I searched around the house for my only help. But perception became a labyrinth of increasing complexity. I was now whispering the names of my loved ones over and over—my identity was being crushed by a blank hammer. I saw the faces that gave meaning to my life abandon their associated names. I was the embodiment of despair. And the glimmer of ego that was left recoiled before the vision of its annihilation. An ethereal light followed every single body in my vicinity. I knew I had minutes to come to terms with the end. But I just felt anger. Why had no one said to me that this was the prelude to death? Why were there no records? Someone touched my shoulder. I was staring at the avenue. "Are you all right?" asked a gruff voice. I had no answer. I saw myself taken by an ambulance into a psychiatric ward. I wished for a speeding car at the distance.

"Seriously, man, how are you feelin'?"

"I did not know I had it in me."

"You eat somethin' from the tray? Don't worry. You'll come down."

"I did not know."

The voice went on blathering and guided me to a room. A burning sensation ran through my spine. I kept thinking I was doomed to this irreversible state. At the threshold of the door, I could distinguish the middle-aged man's silhouette. He walked toward me. He patted my back, put a glass of water near a small table, and withdrew. Here my memory fails. Perhaps I closed my eyes and slept. Perhaps my torturous trip continued.

When I woke up, I was displaced. I ignore whether my readers are familiar with psychosis. Just the same, it is my sincere hope they do not take for granted their marriage to reality. One complete separation is enough never to retrieve the old warmth!

The conversation that ensued I will not judge.

"Hey, I really feel for you. I truly do. But you gotta understand: sometimes we're in a bad place mentally. And that can cause trouble. You're not the first, and you won't be the last."

"Madness is an anecdote? Is that your point?"

"It can't be the grass's fault. Imagine this: you're walking barefoot across the living room and then you step on a little toy truck. Would you blame the truck? Come on, of course not. Maybe you can't even blame yourself. It's the circumstances. Most of the time your living room is safe for your bare feet."

"I looked at the floor. I always look at the floor."

"Maybe you did. Maybe you got distracted."

"This is a mind-altering substance. And these are serious and very unexpected consequences. Have you ever had this happen to you?"

"Not like that. We're all different. You have to relax and ride it out."

"It's pointless. I'm failing to make you understand it. I feel something has been stolen from me."

"What do you want me to tell you? I'm sorry. That's it. That's all I got."

We parted ways.

The sight of the drug soon revolted me. And it was then that I proclaimed a new creed: *Lo mejor de los dados es no jugarlos*. In other words, I joined the tietwats. Their zeal is quite distinct from that of the potheads, for it is a secular zeal—one more fraught with dangers. In religion, there is a place for our nakedness. Not so in the profane province. There we are the alpha and the omega, there we pronounce inexorable judgment. Thus the arable pigments of the exterior devolve into a monochrome dust bowl. Do not deceive yourself, patient reader. The inheritors of Protagoras are legion and await the day every straggling broken-winged thinker has their desiccated corner of the universe!

I fed my righteous bile in conversations with fellow teachers at the nursing school. They were consummate tietwats and had a number of rational (i. e., cold and high-minded) explanations for their disgust. But beneath the façade you could see a life of indoctrination, a life of cautious steps and ambiguous compromises, a life lived with a handkerchief over the forehead.

I will leave my present state to conjecture.[4] I am now called upon by prudence to close my narrative. I

---

[4]"God keep me from ever completing anything."

am aware of its feverish tone. I am aware that in my flights of fancy I have given the impression of vindictive arrogance. Yet I trust the thoughtful reader will have no misgivings. The middle position of which I spoke at the beginning is not one of comfort.

We are proud beings. If we are slavish with the plant, it is in the belief that we are rebelling. For once we are able to choose a world for ourselves, for once we can abandon the fickle sphinx that is reality. If we are contemptuous, it is in the belief that we are obeying. For once we can erect a wall that will keep disruption out, for once we are worthy of our higher demands. What then? I hope the reader will forgive my cryptic answer; I suspect he is in a better condition to dwell on it: we are as the roots of the orchid, children of the air.

Basement Blues

I'VE MADE FRIENDS with dustpans, mops, brooms, buckets, boxes, sprayers 'n rags. Finer than the people upstairs, really. You pass 'em by 'n pray they mind their business. If not, you gotta be prepared to scrub some god-abandoned grime, make-pretend you're the computer guy, do the jack-of-all-trades dance for the suit-wearin' sandal boys or baggy-danglin' barefoot girls, all the while ignorin' their high talk 'n cagey eyes. To hell with those extras. My job's downstairs, mainly alone in shushed company. Mainly, I say, 'cause now 'n then I've to tolerate old Bass, that most poetic of souls, who lets me in on his worn powerful Bible in exchange for naps, God bless 'im. It's a good deal. There's no voice like his nowadays. I swear the fella's punchin' the hundreds. He must be from the times when ladies used artsy large umbrellas 'n the lords strut the streets with canes. Back then if you wanted people to hear ya, you needed the pitch of a cannon. And so I just stare in wonder the nights he preaches. *In the multitude of words there wanteth not sin: but he that refraineth his lips is wise.* You wouldn't find a man that took that more to heart. It's either the Bible or the pillow. The day's holdin' when he spits out his childhood tales. What I wouldn't give to listen to that thunder read the pages from that other Bible. But it's best he steps here once a week. I don't wanna see 'im tired. I try an' fool myself that he's in a nice little house he bought when things were cheap. Yeah, who am I kiddin'? Those are for the pocketswellin' respectables 'n their slips. No rest for the pocket-torn, is what I see.

So I've got plenty hours Tuesdays to Sundays for the cardboard plastic gang. Eight to eight. And let me tell ya: it ain't hard chattin' with your broom or sprayer. It's a damn stick, a damn bottle, but I've seen the respectables talk to their wallet. Don't ya think doin' is best than receivin'? When the boss first hired me, I didn't dream of keepin' company. Twelve hours're no joke. And there was no old Bass. Hard days, hard hard days. But I saw a lady on the sidewalk signin' to 'er plants. She was shinin'. I bet she had young 'uns that forgot they ever had a gramma. What's the difference 'tween a plant 'n some tools, really? Plants just sit there all pretty, waitin' for a shower. The mop's waitin' for a day's duty, no? I'd say that's nicer. So you see me a couple hours later throwin' fresh heartbreak to the boxes. Oh, how they heard me. I was cured. That ain't easy, you know. I'd lost the one girl in the world that could look me in the eye an' say a sweet word. Long story 'n past, so best to forget. I'll confess this many: my 'partment was not mine anymore. I only slept there. Downstairs was my new home. Bigger, cleaner, no rememberin'. Problem was the people upstairs. Bad neighbors still. Always complainin' 'bout the smallest chip. What else? No grand punches 'round 'em. They ain't never got the muscle.

Now I can shoot: no cardboard plastic gang suits me just like the poor dust-collectin' manekwin. Flowers look twisty 'n wild. Tools look heavy 'n past it. But this goodly doll's a charmin' piece o' livin'. I feel best when I've a couple o' wonder stories for it, 'er, whatever. Gotta save 'em. All the borin' cuts go to the others. So if a highfalutin gentlecramp swamps me with broomthrustin' or a la-di-da tobaccopuff hurricanes his ashes, it's the usual. Come on over, friends. You believe this secret boss that's been hidin' all these years? But if a churchdemandin' syrupywinsome hands a winkin' buck, praise the high heavens. The doll's hearin' all 'bout it. I describe the clothes, makeup, colors 'n figure. I describe the weather too. My words're dressed for the party. I don't bother much. Happens twice a year, thrice if the Lord's slot-machines're messed up. He must have some fun, no? Even old Bass knows that. Talkin's it. Difference is 'tween happy 'n the other stuff. I'm not 'bout to hug the doll. I know what's what. I like orderin', that's all. And best to pick circles than squares, is what I say.

I don't need no friends then, no sweetheart, no home. I'm set. I've tried 'em an' they ain't workin'. Friends're for the easy street riders. I had four in my block, but it's like havin' grown baby boys that cry in very strange ways, 'cause you don't see no tears. Hey, lil' Flask, you serious? Where were you? Carin' for the money? What else, bunch o' hoodlums? I take my coin where it blossom right now, an' sure the pocket of our sweaty brothers got no roots. Leave 'em hold to their drownin' families 'n pray. That's gonna need be 'nuff. Who's stormin' the job 'n kickin' out the roly-polies? The doublechin spaniels that make-pretend there's justice outside their doormat? Not ever, my yardbirds. Old Bass with his crumblin' bones? Your lil' Flask, that talk almost with no livin'? We're just a bunch o' ragged bags. Muster a thousand, an' see how three tall kids that been eatin' three meals every day smoke us. Give us a rifle an' you best believe we headin' to the wild, lookin' for some real peace 'tween the pines. It's true, really. I say, then, leave your tired brothers. We're set. When the sun's tryin' for a desert we swat the palms 'n fill trucks o' dates, thinkin' 'bout the sea. When nobody's dyin' for shade we build ritzy roofs, tastin' what it's like. When the lights're flashin' to surprise we clean downstairs week in 'n week out, yammerin' to the crumbs. It don't matter what we make-pretend. We ain't reachin' in this lifetime where the water taste like wine.

Margins

IT'S HARD for me to remember where I heard that sitting close to a corner when alone is far from advisable—something to do with offering an unpleasant sight. Yet here I am, smoking and staring. Next to my table, a pair of teenagers sulk over some trifle about a trip; near them, a disheveled family of three struggle to keep the food from overwhelming their mouths; opposite, two old men play chess while discussing the burden that life becomes; not far, a slick couple, assuming no one is watching because of their respectable appearance, mess around with their hands under the table. They all share what I've not had the opportunity to enjoy.

Many times I've speculated in front of this same cup of coffee, one of the few past its prime, about the reason. And again and again I arrive at the same insurmountable fact: ugliness. It's easy enough to brush aside, but I believe I've been rigorous. This is how it goes.

Average, hard-working people—those are my parents. They know the central privilege of not being a minority; that is, they know a semblance of agency. Pretty fine if you have something going for you.

Otherwise, a bland existence awaits. Sad, but not too sad. They have each other; they have a roof. The life they could offer me was austere. Few words, few surprises, few chances. A life not unlike the one of my neighbors. Except they stumbled upon a shiny little object called hope. When all the children clustered to sing the praises of sport, the mere awareness of my presence suggested a different chant: *Here comes Rickety Robert with his rickety knee, give him a nail and a hammer to help him be*! You might guess the problem. My parents did what they could to improve my knock-knee, but it worsened with the years. Since summers were terribly hot, using shorts was inevitable. And I can't blame the kids for the laughs. Do we not notice a stark contrast in less than a second? Are not children especially prone to comment on differences in less than a second? I was sensitive. I couldn't bear the thought of hearing that chant every time I tried to play with someone else. Kicking a ball toward another kid wasn't that important. A wall was equally effective. I figure each night they were all eager to see each other in the morning. Hope, yes.

School was a slightly different story. We were all welcomed to a haven of sorts. No wonder they grew to be confident even in their mediocrity. They could count on at least one palm to pat their shoulder. I, on the other hand, was met with a mixture of bemusement and pity—owing, surely, to my age. Then the world was not as cruel as it would come to be. Adults in general felt it a responsibility to point to my existence. And this altruistic impulse worked like a patch on threadbare trousers. I'm indebted. It blinded me sweetly to the reality waiting outside.

When you're a small creature, you arouse a curious sense of protectiveness in those around you. It doesn't matter that you're deformed or repulsive. Actually, this helps to exacerbate the feeling. Human beings find the minute inoffensive, and thus have a shot at control. But it all felt quite different in those days. Why ruin the memory? I do have to emphasize, however, that with age comes a bleak change.

In high school, adolescents everywhere are thrown into a miniature version of life. The authority figures here are true to form. They ask something very specific of you; outside it, you can rot. It's at this moment that emotions have their one and only opportunity to develop unhindered. All further displays, I'm positive, are an echo. And so, if you're stifled in any important way, it's a damning affair. I would've appreciated being like the thousands—a speck that collapses with other specks, not a charred remain. But no such privilege was handed. I was made a buffoon, since my body seemed to evidence the suitability of the role. And this I do resent. Ugliness is one of the worst instances of fatalism. You can picture yourself as a lawyer, a painter, a doctor, an actor. But first and foremost you're a blotch. Why deny that we're all physiognomists at heart, the orthodox sons of Lavater?

Dire times, true. Made worse by a lack of focus. I had no consuming passions. My head was as barren as my body. A deliberate choice. I loathed the idea of compensation. To trouble myself with knowledge reeked of spindliness. The examples were profuse: professors humiliating students in the only way left to them, now stripped of youth; professors humiliating other professors in the only way left to them, cloistered as they were in this ascetic environment; students humiliating other students in the only way left to them, physical vigor being unattainable. I wouldn't join them. You can imagine fiction was no relief.

Identifying with protagonists was another insidious form of compensation. Besides, creative acts seemed to me to betray a blighted nature. A fulfilling life is its own end.

Is this the complete truth? Well, no. I would be a hypocrite if I were to portray myself as a guileless pariah. There were frank fellows who approached. But I hadn't the optimism to meet such attempts at friendship. They smiled at things that would never make me smile; they enjoyed a peek beneath the veil that was to me a barrier. I didn't have the secret support of those who boast a disinterested spirit.

You might suspect that here rests the answer, that I could've landed some lifelong friendships and the beautiful camaraderie which follows. You would be mistaken. Without hope there is no defense against the question of questions: why bother? All the airy homilies that fill our vital atmosphere come from people who have temperamental diseases that can be cured through a healthy contact with the community. They're addressed toward ears other than ours.

High school ends. And a life of brooding in loneliness begins. I came across the claims of evolutionary psychology, the claims of religion—bitter tales, though hardly worthy of a category beyond caricature; simplifications with the gloss either of abstract reasoning or revelation. I can understand, however, their appeal. They're ready-made weapons to the pessimist or the optimist. Moreover, they make sense of the fatalism. Behind the aesthetic and moral repulsion lies a story of cunning ancestors who have bred cunning offspring, or a story of a hermetic paternal figure who cares in spite of all evidence to the contrary.

I now have a job as a proofreader in a middling business. I rarely interact with people, as is appropriate.

Margins

And my boss is one of those adults I spoke about; he pities me. But once again I'm indebted. I'm shut off from the stream of wearying life. While I certainly can't dive and bathe like others, exulting in the sun's gentle burn, at least there is a roof above me. And there are windows through which I can feel the breeze and gaze at this perplexing pageant of congealed desires. I almost feel irremediably alienated from them, pure mind.

Almost. Here I am, with a cup of coffee past its prime and a brimming ashtray. The waitress draws closer to my table and smiles what appears to be a dutiful smile. As she cleans the mess, her perfume rouses me from the slumber of self-absorption. I notice a birthmark in her left arm, wrinkles near her eyes, a red flush in her chest. I wish she would acknowledge me without the need of speech, without the protracted efforts. She leaves. I'm suddenly a body. And I'm gasping for breath.

Levity

I

IT SEEMS air finally enters my lungs. I feel the armchair pushing back. I raise a finger, keep it suspended, and find it as robust as a stone bridge. The stupor is clearing. Yet there lingers a despairing distance between morning light and the living room.

I am not ready to leave the armchair, a ballast-turned-coffin these past few days. I guess I should close my eyes and ignore the sudden need for a glass of water, ignore also the appalling silence of the neighborhood. Why did I ever choose this place? Rational choices, alas. An imbecile fad. So what if by the end of a hectic day I was welcomed home with the echoes of childish rapture and teenage angst? Just now I would settle for the creak of a door, white noise, anything that signals other people going on with their routines.

I am not ready for pills. No. It is too late for a defeat of that kind. Dependence should be limited to my cane; dignity has flowered forth after a reluctant struggle. I fear there is no dignity to be found in messy, disincarnate little things.

Seventeen past twelve. If I remain still, so will the minute hand. I have to drink.

Sleep Decades

As I rise, my knees trouble themselves with weight distribution. The luster of the cane, which is close to the door, tempts me. I may falter, but it would be foolish to yield; the physicality of my movements is consoling.

My hand trembles while holding the glass. Someone else could be holding it for me. Another choice, though sensible this time. It is beyond cruel to bind a soul with the purpose of managing domestic inconveniences. Not to speak of begetting assistance. One is enough for the sum of pain to exceed prospects.

I stare at the glass after these sterile musings. A slight, ominous discomfort begins to creep in. I head over to the armchair, agitated by each step.

The door of the bedroom is ajar. Its minor sight awakens a revulsion in the pit of my stomach. I have not slept there in months. All that waits inside, the most meticulous map of a personality, has become mute. When I see the only photograph of my parents, I see a puritanical man who appears uncomfortable in his oversized suit and a severe woman whose skin matches the pale color of her extravagant dress. I am not compelled to recall our moments together. I may as well have the photograph of a random Victorian couple. When I touch the lamp table of my grandfather, I touch a rigid, dust-laden piece of old wood, hardly a comforting token of the days that are no more. Nor do things differ when I look at the carpet, venue of trifling romance.

My knees ache. I must distract myself. For the time being, I am too blank for nostalgia to fashion memory into a warm cabin. I require a jolt.

"Hello?"

Paul's timbre is appropriate.

"Hello."

"Who is this?"

"Victor."

"Victor, huh? Victor . . ."

"The unmarried Victor."

"How about that? This is the first I've heard you over the phone. Quite the deep voice."

"Is it?"

"Sure. I almost thought I'd won a prize. But then I looked at the hour."

"I acted on impulse. I apologize."

"Don't be so stiff."

"Is this the first time I've called you?"

"It is. You never were the talkative type."

"Well, I figured it would be good to catch up. I haven't heard from you or Leslie in a while."

"Leslie has tried getting in touch with you. At least that's what he told me last. If you didn't answer him, why would you answer me? Bah. Excuses. But what the hell. I'm glad to know you're up and about."

"How is everything?"

"Not bad. Usual stuff. Some problems with Viv. I need a hobby. At my age, you can't stay home all day with another person. There's nothing to do."

"I see. That sounds less than ideal."

"Leslie's doing okay. Stand-up guy."

"I'll pick up the phone next time."

"You should. What about you?"

I envisioned a late arrival for this question. Paul has always been prone to long-drawn autobiographical excursus, asking about others purely as a second thought.

"I'm fine."

"Sixty-four years of self-reliant Vic. You'll never stop impressing me."

"It was good hearing from you, Paul."

"You're leaving already? That's not what I would call catching up."

"A strenuous day awaits, I'm afraid."

"Take care. Let's go for a drink later on. Could be the hobby I'm looking for."

I hang up. I do not want the conversation to devolve into a gluttonous recollection of old times. I am not up for the task.

The pain has dulled. My eyes feel heavy.

II

The sound of my neighbor's engine wakes me. Light seeps modestly through the blinds. I must have slept a couple of hours. Instead of letting the living room bathe in overwhelming white while I continue seated, it would be better to walk.

I grab my cane, which now seems unremarkable, and cross the door. The engine's rumble reverberates and finds my sluggish step. I wave to the neighbor, but he is too involved with his car. No one else has bothered going outside. Were it not for the engine, and some stray cuss, yesterday's silence would survive intact.

Near the main avenue, I take a cab. The driver, a man with the face of a boy, awkwardly tries to help me in, although it is clear I need no support. He is polite to a fault. But I talk. I refuse to carry in any way the silence of the neighborhood. As we exchange niceties, I see that his courteous demeanor is rooted in an endearing prejudice: that we old men have a book's worth of wisdom inside ourselves, and thus are entitled to be considered living monuments. I am in no skeptical mood, so I throw around improvised maxims and wait for his wide-eyed glosses. It is quickly time to get out. We are meters from Minerva's witless gaze. Once again, the driver bends over backwards. I thank him.

I stroll through one of the avenues that connects with the roundabout and arrive at an intersection. Here I was denied a meaningful kiss when young. I returned many times, and there was always a trace of that rejection; a trace, however, that grew sweet, for the day it would have to be buried seemed far. And yet it is come. The youths are there, debating, one in favor of abandon, the other against; he hesitates, and she is gone. An incident among thousands to which this intersection bears witness, to which I now bear witness as impersonally.

I feel weightless. The surface of things disappears in a forgiving depth. A mixture of mature exuberance and infantile despair seizes me. I do not know what to do with it. I walk in a daze and endure wave after wave of uncertainty.

I am ushered home, celebratory at last.

III

The wrinkles are abyssal and ubiquitous, as if they were the ripples a rock thrown at the bridge of the nose had formed; the eyes, slits subjugated by hispid eyebrows; the nose, a skewed protuberance; the mouth, a fissure. It seems fitting.

Spillage surrounds the oxfords. I turn off the faucet. The bathtub receives my body with obduracy. Not so the water. As I submerge, the embrace brings peace. Room for thought broadens. I am granted a glimpse of the future. Paul and Leslie sit in a bar. They listen to my story of the cabdriver. They are amused, they hope to meet him. Before long, we speculate about his hardships. A wonderful night. I have no stories left within me. Nor am I eager for more. After an outstretched silence, it is good to see the world bid farewell in jest.

τὸ ὄν

Have you heard the double waves?

What?

Listen.

I only hear the waves.

They are there. They are not hidden.

the first to spill, the first to hint beyond the concept that wreathes them

the first, yes, the first, they bear miracles, the palpable boundless

a kid one feels like before them, a kid then a bundle of disjointed thoughts

the first to surround you and instill awe and disquiet and whatever else is sublime

and you notice
one crashes
then the other
then another
then others
anothers
many

how
briskly
just one
not many
not an echo
afterthought
and you notice

How are you?

I . . . is he still here?

Fabrizio?

The dog.

Yes, Fabrizio. He is here.

Fabrizio.

you look dignified, aware, much more aware than anyone here

is it inconceivable that you understand in your way?

is it inconceivable to think you a victim of some hurried cast done from afar and extended beyond its use like most we deem serviceable and then find a trap?

in a caress i confirm the suspicion

a victim and still you stray among us

with you, there is no fundamental loneliness

stay
stay please stay
you do not seem lost
i on the other hand
and not just now
in general
stay

Well. You should look at yourself.

Where is he going?

You are covered in sand.

Can you call him?

He follows anyone who passes by.

I need him here. With us.

I am sure he answers to no one.

the brightness, has it always been here, possibly

no, im sure, otherwise what illusion

its here and if only one noticed, what remedy

will darkness be as bright

it must, it persists in its place, all that persists in its place is bright

the sky holds every color and for it to do so it must
strain immeasurably

why are the tracts between things so immense

andallthesandallthesandpushingagainstthe
              agitation of the sea the grand impatience

but time, the most puzzling, why does it stand still
is it to retain this extravagance
can it

please, Clara, talk to me.

I'm here.

i need you to talk to me.

What is it?

it's just that silence feels eternal

I'm here. You're fine. They'll come back.

the sun understands about placement, what touch in
its care for the grace of her contour

painters are mere toddlers we all are mere toddlers,
who take a babble as some nearness to this grace yet i
understand our confusion, deliberate perhaps

there they come as graceful as delicately sketched

how can one not love all that participates in this
rapture of constant birth

when that particular lifting of sand, when that
labyrinth of drops sticking in the whole of their bodies
when the direction in which her hair is being blown
when the cadence of this laughter when the rhythm
of this touch, when

nature is a spendthrift
i dont see any care
it gives and gives
knows no waiting
all anew
swept
away
and yet
furthers

There is the sparkle in the eyes.

Think he can handle the ocean?

Yes. Everything is in its place.

He looks like a child.

Part of it. Let's go.

step by step

how soothing the way water surrounds my soles then
heels then feet then ankles then calves then knees
then thighs then hips to think a vast turmoil would
have care strewn through the whole of its span so that
any pulse of life could immerse in its presence

step by step

the waves crash close and i get the hints of more than
this they crash and make light trembles of me they
crash and im just my body they crash and theres not
much more

step by step

i know to go no further theres no voice that brings
this thought this is no voice its a body

isnt it

each purported syllable spaces itself when turned outward

nice to

and i see eternity between

feel the waves

an anomaly that is

crash against you

consciousness that is

isnt it

i lose voice amid such pauses

almost

i dont know whether theyll hear

overwhelming

whatever it is that comes out

am i making sense is there a net between us so that i
traverse wide thoughts here while a single consonant
fizzles over there so that no complete thought reaches
far i fear i dont

i see no reaction or at least none that matches
whatever it is i would say why is there a net and if
there isnt why do i feel so pronounced a contrast in
the inner and outer rhythms

the sky blends a rich palette of oranges and violets and
blues and somehow the precise luster of the waves is a
perfect match and i feel tempted to call it the same
matter

the waves increase their dissolving against me and i
am losing the notion of our distinctness i am losing
my boundaries i am drifting in and out in and out
until all solves itself in color

why the stare whats wrong tell me

                                                    go on

why are you worried

                                 I am not you can be sure

i need to know

                              it is nothing look at the sunset

im unwell

            come on let's get out of the water and join Clara

why am i chained to my thoughts to this one filter

that leaks and is crooked

i know too much about its outline

name

                                                                                            this

birth

                                                                                            that

occupation

                                                                                         other

goal

                                                                  this other

i need out

name

birth

occupation

goal

we'll catch up with you
is he okay
yes it's a part of
we could all go together
he needs some air
all right

their faces distort contort involute convolute
and all is time
i no longer have
particulars
aside from
movement

let's give them some advantage
how do you feel
breathe everything comes to that
breathe and do not outpace it

music can lead when you are lost have you noticed it has always been so for me i assume it must relate to its deft play with ephemerality and transcendence nothing else approaches it literature has a deadened quality of which it cannot get rid imagination must enliven the page it thus participates of transcendence sculpture and painting have a presence that somehow gets us closer to the ephemeral but it falls short and so on music lilts through time awakens our senses in a trance lives in spite of ourselves try to impose an image and you are sure to miss its pleasures our sole laugh at transience see the waves they move inexorably toward an indifferent coast but what dance they make of it we would not be able to count the patterns traced what do we make of our lives not something as dissimilar yet i perceive that only in our pains do we close in on such richness exquisite in the tortures we concoct for ourselves and each other almost fractal in the observance of our pain are not the arts an infinitesimal testament to this where is joy there is a mystery there is the elusive aspect of our texture it seems as alien to us as the light of this sunset is to the waves it reaches they coexist sure but they coexist at wondrous intervals and some waves there are which will know nothing of its blessings i choose not to lament just look at the whole from which a wave is born i count it as imposing as the sun and yet the sun will never participate of its embrace mysteries that is what the brightness amounts to the shade is prosaic complex yes fluent yes malleable yes but prosaic be there art be there companionship be there what you will i find no use then in blabbering about the immaculate nothing of the philosophers we have much to distract us and elevate us and in the end perhaps most is unapproachable as the sun will know nothing of a circling blue so we will know nothing of whatever there is that has its untraceable orbit even if we make a difference to it no symmetry in pain and joy no real *stop* did i ever tell you about the anthropology student i met here *no* it was uncalled for and sudden like most things that matter i guess every afternoon i have been going outside for some coffee and working until sunset this particular day was crowded with families and couples so i had to wait for a table before long i saw her standing we made eye contact and maybe she sensed i had no problem sharing the table with her she asked of course and we were silent at first then i made some small talk surprisingly fluent we were laughing and soon felt compelled to stroll through the coast you know the sunsets here moving there was hesitation and then contact we had fun but it came to an end i accompanied her to her cabin do not ask me why i asked for a photo she said forget just forget and left *sounds ideal* i am not sure it was nonetheless pleasant and i am grateful

violet streak that turns orange and toward the horizon
spills over as pink

blue flowers in the borders as the leaden white
disintegrates in black

ominous ominous ominous ominous even when full of
resplendence

the coast follows in the fragility of a sigh each speck
of sand gone

all that oscillates within is mirrored all within is
blown aside

im scared

we are close you simply have to keep walking

there are so many lights where are we

this is the coast and those are tourists you love the coast

im scared i feel were not getting any closer

you feel that way because its night

oh

we will drink some wine and relax once we are there

i think im coming back

breathe

yes im coming back

just breathe

i feel better much better

the sand feels great no

its passing away

good

i think im coming back

you will

there want to go there
light artificial people a lightbulb parting dark
its not a net more like glass dread for it to mist
when it mists the malaise spreads translucent
it will be easier to walk ten minutes at most
strange that place is taken for granted
all the unmerciful detail ignored
no twice said the bearded one
are you back then
not before
not now

multitudes mumble and jam every conceivable outlet

gathering   dispersing

filling the air with cries laughter complaints

                                      leaving no real distance

                    and the faces just folds and folds of strain

metamorphoses left to be figured by someone or other

        involuntary excrescences of emotion that ordered
                                                                would answer

fear the snake that lurks   between the spectacles

fear the thing that stems   dim empathy

fear the that which gluts   recall

sanity how thin a thread tenuous as a film of water self-willed through increasing remnants of opaque moments that conceal any wish for a consistent now

now where does the street lead but an asylum resigned as the feet feel burdened as the shoulders bow trailing as the thoughts lose the settled path

where to go if refusal blooms unasked if there is yet a part that goes one two three four

do you feel better
what happened back there
always why were you afraid
i see what is the point again it escapes me
losing your grip on things rather counterintuitive

                                          yes
                    emotions sculpted perception
            no the coast disappeared in melancholy hues
                                   experience
                              you dont lose it

its heightened
its as if you were let loose in time
unrestricted by narrative demands
playful with the porousness of apprehension

dislodgement from memory
is close to an unraveling
a lifetime of misdeeds may pass
or a fateful minute that holds a bitter account

Let us set the wine the bread the cheese the butter
Come hold the bottle and throw away the apple
Dont be too cautious it will not slip your grasp
Come the evening is moving
You are here you are with us
Grab a seat and enjoy
Spread the butter
Taste

it is a choreography

                                        the setting of plates

                                        the calculated smiles

the measured insistence on sanity

                                        the filling of cups

                                        the considerate glances

the salient limp to assuagement

to try

to try

but it is no use   for one who loses taste

                                                      at sight

                                                      at sight

                the arms the legs the hands

              how foreign to the wistful eyes

the breeze unconveyed
a light in the center iridescent
crumbs atop crumbs

time
trickles
as
patient
stream

the chatter mutes into efflorescence
theres a light in the center bright oblique
the surroundings grow haze
i am not here

Touch.

The hand that instantiates two distinct pulses through the perceptual kaleidoscope.

I am crushing a shell.

Patterned so as to incite the thought of other more complex pulses in parallel.

Vibration.

There is a trailing blur that seems foreign, alternating its appearance to the rhythm of my breath.

i am unable to recover coherence

my lucidity is up to the breath
exasperating in its syncopations

there is at least a gradual feel
for the limits of my body

proprioception is slack

where now

Claras gone

Mateos gone

Ezers brooding

i wouldnt like to repeat myself

                                                                                     whats that

i do believe im approaching the end

                                                                                 its been rough

guilty

                                            no it would be pointless

there are these long pauses in which i get scared

                                                                                    why

the shadow of incoherence

                                                                            go on

a lot happens inside my head its terrible not knowing what goes out

                                                        your words tell much

about

                                                        in out you know its over

i dont believe it is
even your eyes are telling
i can focus them
yes they are no longer prey
to what
incoherence
i guess most things are ordered now
it is a vague term
well the experience is vague
you will come to realize it is not

there's this persistent anxiety underneath

is it related to the incoherence

yes, everything's related to it

i didn't know you feared insanity this much

wouldn't you, anyone

out of a misunderstanding

that's pure extravagance

no, there is a misunderstanding

believing control over our whole being is desirable

something like it, yes

the thoughts of a wayward son, truly

whatever there is underneath, to put it your way, can be trusted

it strikes me more as tragedy, just remember the homeless

always look to the eyes, there is a glimmer to which we have no real access

and there is a very real pain too

i readily grant that, but the pains and joys of the unhinged are of another kind

we are all, finally, beings with a nervous system

your materialism seems intact, in a way, but you miss the point

insanity, madness, resides in a physical change

i wouldn't argue otherwise, the case stands, our knowledge of mechanism is precarious

the sky wobbles still.

it is a dilated, leisured landing.

it has been. only when the sky ceases to be a net i'll know.

what do you make of all these apparitions?

you just said it. my materialism has suffered no actual blow.

i have to insist with the question.

all apparitions had their springboard in perceptible objects, more or less.

you haven't been forward with them.

take the majestic glow of things. it depended on the sun, a source of light. there's also the disintegration of the coast. it obeyed my mood.

so an actual blow would have consisted in a brand new reality dawning upon you.

yes, not a heightened version of this one, however spasmodic.

a peeling off of a layer?

perhaps.

that was what happened, no?

you could argue it did, but the limit was clear.

how do you mean?

i was not about to be transported into Coleridge's Xanadu.

how do you feel right now?

mildly disoriented, but better.

can you treat a delicate subject?

probably.

When we were dining, you were suddenly paralyzed. I have rarely seen anyone in that state.

I recall.

Your face was disassembled by fear. Hardly a human face for a second.

I was losing all of you.

Losing us?

In the vortex of thoughts, some shipwrecked conceit made me believe we had been stranded for weeks owing to my psychosis. Then I saw a light and realized we were not here.

Dire.

It is perhaps the most hopeless I have felt in my life.

Give me the materialist account.

You say to yourself again and again, "This is temporal, this is temporal." But there comes a moment when everything is too vivid, too confusing, too dream-like. You adjust. Or try to, anyway. And then you have to readjust. In these oscillations a break is bound to happen. Was that the only point at which you were on the verge?

Yes.

You were also out of your depth on the beach, close to evening.

Right, right.

A break?

Of a different order.

Your unalloyed skepticism in the middle of two breakdowns is equally bold and baffling.

Unalloyed? No, no.

Why of a different order?

There was bliss.

"I think we're talking about different instants."

"While in the ocean, I became the singular clash between rays of sunset and foam."

"And yet."

"Perhaps we're too frail to sustain intensity of perception."

"Unalloyed."

"This is how far I would go: memory, with enviable skill, weaves a tapestry that encloses our wilful emotional life; in moments of unsurmountable agitation, be they breakdowns or psychotic lapses, the tapestry is rent, the emotions disperse, the outer is caught erratically yet isn't synthesized; there is no you for the time being. I suspect the fabric can be irreversibly damaged."

"So our experience of the divine is just that, the loss of identity."

"Yes. In the hurried reconstructions of our bearings, we invent that entity which will account for the alluvion."

"A curious, feeble reductionism. Grandeur demoted to psychological casuistry. I always fear tidiness in these matters."

"I know I'm simplifying."

"What after the rending of the tapestry?"

"I didn't mention it, but to one not inclined toward religion there is still interpretation."

The waves suggest more.

Listen.

Something is there, discreet.

Listen and breathe.

Something mine.

Other Titles from Malarkey

Faith, a novel by Itoro Bassey
The Life of the Party Is Harder to Find Until You're the Last One Around, poems by Adrian Sobol
Music Is Over, a novel by Ben Arzate
Toadstones, stories by Eric Williams
Deliver Thy Pigs, a novel by Joey Hedger
It Came From the Swamp, edited by Joey Poole
Pontoon, an anthology of fiction and poetry
What I Thought of Ain't Funny, edited by Caroljean Gavin
Guess What's Different, essays by Susan Triemert
White People on Vacation, a novel by Alex Miller
Your Favorite Poet, poems by Leigh Chadwick,
Sophomore Slump, poems by Leigh Chadwick
Man in a Cage, a novel by Patrick Nevins
Fearless, a novel by Benjamin Warner
Don Bronco's (Working Title) Shell, a novel? by Donald Ryan
Un-ruined, a novel by Roger Vaillancourt
Thunder From a Clear Blue Sky, a novel by Justin Bryant
Kill Radio, a novel by Lauren Bolger
The Muu-Antiques, a novel by Shome Dasgupta
Backmask, a novel by OF Cieri
Gloria Patri, a novel by Austin Ross

Where the Pavement Turns to Sand,
stories by Sheldon Birnie
Still Alive, a novel by LJ Pemberton
I Blame Myself But Also You, stories by Spencer Fleury
Hope and Wild Panic, stories by Sean Ennis
Thumbsucker, poems by Kat Giordano
The Great Atlantic Highway & Other Stories,
by Steve Gergley
First Aid for Choking Victims,
stories by Matthew Zanoni Müller
Boxcutters, stories by John Chrostek
Hair Shirt, poems by Adrian Sobol

Death of Print Titles

Consumption & Other Vices, a novel by Tyler Dempsey
Awful People, a novel by Scott Mitchel May
Drift, a novel by Craig Rodgers
The Ghost of Mile 43, a novel by Craig Rodgers
One More Number, stories by Craig Rodgers
Francis Top's Grand Design, stories by Craig Rodgers
Francis Top's Lost Cipher, stories by Craig Rodgers

malarkeybooks.com

www.ingramcontent.com/pod-product-compliance
Lightning Source LLC
LaVergne TN
LVHW041931070526
838199LV00051BA/2773